A Twist of Fortune

BARBARA MITCHELHILL

ANDERSEN PRESS
LONDON

First published in 2013 by
Andersen Press Limited
20 Vauxhall Bridge Road
London SW1V 2SA
www.andersenpress.co.uk

British Library Cataloguing in Publication Data available.

ISBN 978 1 849 39562 5

Printed and bound by CPI Group (UK) Ltd, Croydon, CR0 4YY

For Louise, Lucy, Max and Tom

One

First Home

I'm Sam Pargeter and this is my story. When it began, I was nearly twelve. By the time it ended, I was fourteen. So you see, it's a long story and some bad things happened on the way – just to warn you in case you worry about stuff like that.

It started the day Pa told us his news. We were all there in the cottage, Ma, Eliza, Alfie and me. Sitting at the table. Listening to what he said. He told us with a big grin on his face as if it was a joke – but it wasn't. My stomach jolted and the hairs stood up on the back of my neck. I knew things were going to be different now.

Before that day, I thought nothing would ever change. I thought we'd live in the country for ever. Pa would work on Mister Garwood's farm, and Eliza and me would help with the hay in summer and scare the crows in spring. Though we were as poor as church mice, it was a grand life. We liked chasing rabbits and climbing trees and looking for birds' eggs. Even Eliza, who was only ten, could climb the biggest trees. Not many girls could do that, but she could.

'Watch me, Sam,' she'd say. And she'd shin up the trunk of

1

an oak in a flash, not caring if she got into trouble for tearing her frock.

Alfie was just four years old and Ma spoiled him something rotten. Maybe it was cos baby Henry had died some years back. Ma cried a lot then, I remember. She cried really hard when we put him in the tiny box Pa made and buried him in the churchyard. I made a little wooden cross and carved 'Henry' on it and we picked buttercups and laid them by it. It was a sad day.

A year after that, Alfie was born. We all thought he was special and Ma stopped crying and smiled again and everything was happy.

I won't pretend our cottage was grand. It wasn't much bigger than a garden shed built of brick and rotting timber and, when it rained, water dripped through the thatch right into the house.

'Well, blow me down, that's a lucky thing,' Ma would say. 'No need to fetch water from the well, my loves.'

While the rain dripped into a bucket, me and our Eliza would sit by the fire, Alfie would settle on Ma's knee and she'd tell us stories. I loved Ma's stories. They were full of magical places and adventure. My favourite was about Aladdin, the boy with the magic lamp. Ma always said he had bright blue eyes like me and Pa, and he could run like the wind just like my sister, and he had curls like Alfie. But I don't reckon Aladdin had red hair like us.

Sometimes, on rainy days, Pa would teach us reading and writing. He knew about books, see, because he'd been to school when he was young. He tried to teach Ma too but she wasn't so interested. Pa had three books he kept on the shelf and most days he'd read to us after tea. One was the Bible bound in black leather with gold lettering and the other two were stories by Charles Dickens. We all liked *Pickwick Papers* cos it was very funny.

'Do that silly voice for Mister Pickwick, Pa,' Eliza would say, and he'd pinch his nose between his fingers and speak all high-pitched so that we rocked with laughter.

My favourite was *Oliver Twist* which was about a poor orphan who got into terrible trouble. A thief called Fagin taught Oliver to steal and Pa did a scary voice for him and made us shiver and Alfie would say, 'Bad man. Bad man.'

I expect you're wondering that if life was so good, what did Pa say that shocked me so much and changed everything. Well, I'll tell you. That day we thought Pa had gone to work on the farm as usual, but he came back early and said he had something to tell us. Ma made a pot of tea, looking nervous I thought – though I didn't know why she should. We all settled round the table wondering what the news could be.

'It's like this,' Pa said. 'The harvest wasn't good last year and Mister Garwood can't afford to pay me. So his son, Jacob, will work on the farm instead.'

'That's not fair,' said Eliza.

'Not fair,' Alfie repeated, which made Pa laugh.

'Jacob will be thirteen next week,' said Pa, 'and he's a strong lad. He'll be a good worker.'

'What will you do, Pa?' I asked.

He grinned and winked at us. But he didn't fool me. I could tell that deep down he wasn't happy.

'I'm glad you asked, Sam,' he said. 'Today I went to see a friend of Mister Garwood's who's a wealthy man with business in foreign parts.' He leaned forward and tried to make his smile even wider. 'So I'm going on an adventure!'

'Can we come?' Eliza asked.

'I'm afraid not, sweetheart. It's just me.'

Eliza's face fell and Pa put his hand on hers.

'I'll be sailing to America, you see,' Pa said. 'It's a big country with lots of open spaces and amazing wild animals. I'll be able to tell you all about it when I come back. That's exciting, isn't it?'

But it wasn't exciting. It was horrible! I didn't want him to go away. Eliza must have felt the same because she leaped out of her chair and flew into one of her tempers, screaming and yelling, which set Alfie off crying.

'No, no, no! You can't leave us!' she bawled, thumping Pa's chest with her fists.

He wrapped his arms around her and held her tight, trying to calm her down. 'I have to go, my chicken. I need to earn money. We have to eat, don't we?'

'I'm nearly twelve,' I said. 'Why can't I get a job?'

'You're not old enough to do man's work, son. If I go to America, I'll earn good money for us all.'

Well, it didn't sound right to me. 'That's daft,' I said. 'How's leaving us going to help?'

Pa sat down, pulling Eliza, still sobbing, onto his knee. 'I'm going to America to grow cotton.'

'You mean you'll be a farmer?'

'I'll be a boss man in charge of cotton fields. I'll send money home to Ma and I'll work hard and I'll soon be rich. Then I'll come back.'

'Well, that's a lucky thing,' said Ma, trying to be brave. 'You'll be home before we know it.' But I could tell she was upset because I saw her wipe away a tear when she thought we weren't looking. I expect she'd known what Pa was planning but it was a terrible shock for Eliza and me. Alfie was too young to understand, see.

Eliza sniffed back her tears. 'Will you be back next week?' she asked. I thought that was a stupid thing to say. I knew America was a long way away. Over the sea. Miles and miles from home – he wouldn't even be halfway there in a week.

Pa kissed her forehead. 'Not so soon,' he said. 'I'll be back in a year or so, my pet. Perhaps.'

That set her off howling and hollering so bad that Alfie, who didn't know what was going on, got scared and joined in.

'Aww! What a terrible noise, my loves!' said Ma, pulling a face and shaking her head. 'Shall we have a nice noise instead?' Which is what she always said when we were arguing or making a fuss. Then she started singing with a voice as sweet as a lark. Eliza loved to sing too, and her voice was just like Ma's. After getting her crying under control, she joined in and the two of them sang 'Daisy's Dimples' while the rest of us listened.

'Beautiful,' said Pa, settling in his chair to light his pipe. 'That's the most beautiful sound in the whole world.'

The day came when Pa had to leave. He took me to one side and said, 'While I'm away, Sam, I want you to look after Ma and your sister and brother. You'll be twelve soon. Can you be the man of the house, do you think? Can you manage that?'

Part of me wanted to say, 'Course, I can. I can do it.' But part of me wanted to scream, 'Don't leave us, Pa! Don't go!' All I did was nod my head and say, 'I'll manage.'

Later, we stood at the gate as Pa set off for America to make his fortune.

'Be good, all of you. Make sure you read to them, Sam,' he called as he walked away down the lane. 'I'll write as soon as I get there.'

And he lifted his hand and waved to us and we waved back until he was over the brow of the hill and out of sight.

Two

Letters

We missed Pa something shocking. We missed him reading to us and telling jokes and laughing with us. I did my best to help Ma and look after the others. I dug the vegetable patch in front of the house and chopped wood. Eliza fetched the water from the well, fed the hens and collected the eggs. But it wasn't easy without Pa.

Then one day – it was months later – Eliza came running into the cottage clutching a small package, wrapped in brown paper and tied with string. It was addressed to Missus Annie Pargeter.

'Ma!' yelled Eliza. 'See what I've got!'

Ma, who was was making bread, looked up.

'I think it's from Pa,' said Eliza as she put it on the table while Alfie and me gathered round, bursting to see what Pa had sent us.

'Well, now,' said Ma, wiping the flour from her hands. 'I wonder what this can be.' And she smiled at us as we all waited for her to unwrap it. First she undid the string, rolled it into a ball and put it on the shelf.

'Quick, Ma,' I said. 'We want to see what's inside.'

She grinned, looking as excited as I felt and she pulled off the brown paper. Inside was a small leather pouch with a drawstring top. Alfie grabbed it as if it was a toy and ten silver coins fell out onto the table. We were all amazed at the sight of them.

'It's treasure, Ma!' said Eliza.

She picked up one of the coins and turned it over in her hand. 'It's Pa's treasure! He's sent us American money,' she explained. 'I'll have to ask Mister Garwood to take it to his bank and change it into pounds.'

Just as Pa had promised, there was a letter in the package.

'Read it, Sam,' said Ma, her cheeks flushed pink with excitement.

I read it out loud – not once but three times, which pleased Ma no end. America was very hot, Pa said, but he was working hard and saving his money so he could come home. He said how much he missed us, which made Ma cry – but in a happy sort of way. She put the letter in the little silver box Pa had given her when they got married and set it on the shelf next to Pa's books.

'It'll be safe there,' she said.

There was a return address on Pa's letter so, that afternoon, I set about writing to him telling him all the things we'd been doing and begging him to hurry home cos we missed him. Eliza did a drawing of our house with us all standing in the garden with silly grins on our faces and we put Alfie's sticky hand print right at the bottom. Ma didn't know much about writing so she did a row of kisses which would make Pa really happy.

A month later, just after my twelfth birthday, another package arrived, exactly the same – some silver coins and a letter from Pa. We were just as excited as before and we were glad to hear that the cotton was growing well and it would soon be time to pick it. The letter was put into the silver box along with the first one, and we were happy to know all was going well.

After that, I thought the letters would come regular. But when another month passed and nothing came, I was worried. We all were. I went down the lane to meet the postman and I asked him to look in his sack. But he shook his head. No packets. No letters for the Pargeter family.

Weeks passed. Months passed. The money Pa had sent us was gone now. What Ma earned from taking in washing was only just enough to pay the rent. And though Eliza and me went picking stones off Mister Garwood's fields, he didn't pay well so there was not much money for food. We'd had no eggs ever since the fox got into the hen coop and killed the chickens. So we ate cabbages and potatoes mainly and, as time went by, we grew skinny.

The terrible thing was that we didn't know whether Pa was dead or alive. I'd heard there were bad diseases in America, and there was sure to be dangerous animals like lions and tigers so I worried about him all the time. Ma must have been thinking the same and worrying about it too; she began to waste away, see. The months passed and her chubby cheeks and dimples disappeared, her arms became thin as broomsticks. Even her hair faded to grey so it wasn't red like ours any more. From morning till night she looked weary and sad – too tired to sing. Too tired to smile, most of the time.

It was a year since Pa had gone to America. Ma got so bad that we brought the bed downstairs and set it in the corner not far from the fire so she'd be warm. She lay with her eyes closed and her face paler than milk, too weak to get up.

Day by day, she grew worse. Me and Eliza took turns to sit with her, hoping she would get better, but we were sick with fear that she might not. One night, when I was sitting by her bed, she said, 'Sam,' in a voice no louder than the squeak of a mouse.

'What is it, Ma?' I said and put my ear close to her mouth so that I could hear her.

'Write…a letter…to your Aunt Maud,' she gasped. 'Ask her…to come…please.'

She told me what to write. I had to tell her sister that she was ill and wanted to see her and then she fell asleep, exhausted.

Three days later, we were all sitting by her bed. I was reading her favourite bit from *Oliver Twist*. It was the part where Oliver is saved from going to prison by Mister Brownlow who is really kind and takes care of him. Ma liked that a lot.

But before I'd finished, there was a hammering at the door. It took us a while to get up from Ma's bedside and, when we didn't answer straight away, the door was flung open and a woman marched in, dressed from head to toe in black and as skinny as a lugworm. I'd seen her once before when I was only five or so. But I hadn't forgotten that miserable face and those tight lips. Ma always said I shouldn't be frightened of her and that really, deep down, she was kind. But she didn't look it to me.

'Who are you?' demanded Eliza not having seen her since she was very small. 'Why are you bursting in like that?'

I hadn't talked about the letter Ma asked me to write. I didn't want to worry her, see.

'I'm your Aunt Maud, child. Your mother's sister. Where is she?'

'Here,' I said, pointing behind me where Ma was lying in the bed, not even stirring. Hardly breathing now. 'She's sick. We have to talk quiet.'

Aunt Maud glanced over at Ma, took off her hat and laid it on the table. Then she looked at Eliza. 'Can you make tea, child?' she asked.

'I can,' Eliza replied.

'Then make me a cup. I've come a long way today. And take one to your Uncle Bert. He's waiting outside on the cart. Hurry, girl!'

Eliza frowned. I knew she was thinking that our aunt needed to watch her manners – but she didn't say anything. She just looked at me, puzzled as she went to sort out the tea. When it was brewed, she did as she was told and took a cup outside to our uncle. Alfie and me followed so that Aunt Maud could talk to Ma in private like sisters do.

Uncle Bert was in the lane, sitting high up on an old cart, his face red and sweaty from the drive. He wore a shabby top hat and a faded brown suit, which was too tight to button.

'What's going on?' he said, as we handed him the tea. 'How long is she going to be in there?'

There wasn't so much as 'Hello,' or 'How you've grown,' or 'You look like your pa, you do.' Which is what most people say when they haven't seen children for a while. But there wasn't even a smile or a 'Thank you,' for the tea.

'Go and tell her to hurry up,' he said when he'd drained his cup. 'Visiting family is all very well, but I can't be long. I've got a business to run.'

I wish we'd gone back into the house right then. I wish we'd said goodbye to Ma and kissed her. But we didn't. We stood there as Aunt Maud came striding out, her face grim, her lips pressed together.

'We got here just in time, husband,' she called. 'My sister's gone and died.'

Three

Moving on

We knew Ma was sick but we never thought she'd leave us. Not really.

Aunt Maud said they'd stay to arrange the funeral, but Uncle Bert did nothing but grumble, wanting to get back to Camden. It all happened in double quick time and when Ma's poor body was bundled into a rough coffin and taken to the churchyard, I thought my heart would break. Though I tried to be as cheerful as I could for Eliza and Alfie.

As we set out to the churchyard, Eliza whispered, 'I'm taking this with me, Sam.' She pulled back her shawl and there was Ma's silver box tucked under her arm. 'I want to put it in the ground with Ma. Don't want Uncle Bert to see it. I don't trust him.'

I didn't either, but I shook my head. 'You can't do that. It's all we've got to remember Ma by – she'd want us to keep it.'

I was glad she agreed and she tucked the box under her shawl away from Uncle Bert's prying eyes.

Ma was buried next to baby Henry, just like she would have wanted. It was very sad. We all stood round the grave, sobbing and crying and wishing Pa was there. Aunt Maud stood next to the vicar, her face as miserable as ever. It was hard to know if she was sad about Ma, or if that was her only expression. Uncle Bert didn't come. Not that we wanted him to. He stayed back at the house.

When we returned, I was shocked to see our belongings – Pa's books, the pans and kettles, blankets and, worst of all, Ma's clothes – all tossed in a heap onto the cart.

'What are you doing?' I said running up to Uncle Bert. 'You can't take them. They're ours.' But he just shrugged his shoulders and said nothing, and I was glad my sister had the silver box. At least that was safe.

Eliza was angry too. 'Put 'em back,' she yelled. 'You're a thief, you are!'

Aunt Maud grabbed hold of her arm. 'Calm down, child. We can't leave your belongings here. You're coming with us. Your mother asked me to take care of you all.'

'Ma didn't say nothing to us.'

'It was her dying wish,' Maud snapped. 'You're coming home with us.'

'This is our home,' said Eliza. 'We ain't going with you. We're staying.'

Alfie repeated, 'We're staying,' and stamped his foot.

Aunt Maud took no notice. But Uncle Bert said, 'I have a fine business in Camden, you ungrateful child. Very respected, I am, and we have a home in the best part of town.'

'Well, I don't care,' said Eliza. 'I like it here.'

'We like it here,' said Alfie and stuck out his tongue at him.

Uncle Bert was in no mood to hang around. 'Don't waste time,' he snapped at Aunt Maud. 'Get 'em into the cart, if they're coming with us. I've got to be on my way.'

I went and stood in front of him. 'We already said we don't want to go. I'm twelve and I can look after us. Beg yer pardon, Uncle Bert, but we're staying here and that's that.'

Uncle Bert glowered at me from under his top hat. 'Oh, you's staying here, is yer? And who's going to pay the landlord when he comes asking for his rent? Tell me that. Am I going to pay? No I am not, mister. So where will you get the money from, eh?'

I hadn't thought of the rent. I hadn't thought how I'd earn money for food or for clothes when ours wore out or we grew bigger. I hadn't thought.

Uncle Bert leaned back against the cart. 'Life's hard,' he said. 'But you don't want to finish up in the workhouse, does yer?'

'Workhouse' was a terrible word. We'd heard stories about it from people in the village and read about it in *Oliver Twist*. How families were separated. How people were made to break up rocks or pick oakum all day until their fingers bled. It was like prison – only you'd done nothing wrong, except be poor. They took you in and kept you in. None of us wanted to end up in a place like that.

I pulled Eliza and Alfie closer to me. We all stared at Uncle Bert and shook our heads.

'So if you don't want to go to the workhouse, you'll come with me,' he said, slapping his hand on the horse's rump.

'I'll have no trouble finding work for yer all. Especially a lad like you,' he said, nodding in my direction. I knew he was right.

'What about Pa?' asked Eliza, her cheeks wet with tears. 'He won't know where we are.'

I put my hand on her shoulder. 'Don't worry, Eliza. We'll leave him a note.' And I went into the house to find some paper.

This is what I wrote:

DEAR PA,
WE'VE GONE WITH AUNT MAUD AND UNCLE BERT.
PLEASE COME AND FETCH US WHEN YOU GET HOME.

SAM, ELIZA, AND ALFIE.

I pinned it on the door and then we walked down the path and climbed into Uncle Bert's cart.

Four

Mister Bagstone's gentleman's hat shop

We bounced and bumped along in the back of that cart until we were black and blue from it. It took hours to get to Camden and by the time we did, my legs and bum were covered in bruises. But the worst thing was Uncle Bert, who was sitting up front. As soon as we'd left our home, he perked up and seemed as happy as a dog with two tails to be heading back to Camden. Then he never stopped talking all the way.

'Camden is a grand town – real grand,' he said. 'It's not many miles from London and it'll soon have its own railway station. Imagine that, eh? I bet you kids have never seen one o' them new fangled trains, have yer?' He didn't give us a chance to answer, he just yakked on. 'There's fine houses in Camden – oh yes – and shops galore. And I have a splendid business. Though I say it myself, it is the best. The very best for miles around!'

Eliza looked at me and pulled a face. Alfie grinned and started to open and close his mouth like a fish, imitating

Uncle Bert's chatter. Then we began to laugh – we couldn't help it – and clapped our hands over our mouths so he wouldn't hear.

He carried on and on and on. 'I work from morning till night. Morning till night – and that's a fact. I have great plans, you see, and I'll be very rich one day. Oh yes. Very very rich.'

My ears were ringing by the time the cart drove into Camden and I was glad to have something to look at and take my mind off that chatterbasket.

I'd never been in a town, see. I'd always lived in the country so I couldn't help staring as we drove along, my eyes as big as pigeons' eggs. For one thing there were lots of carts on the road. Not hay carts like Mister Garwood had on his farm. These carts were carrying all kinds of things like metal bars and planks of wood and sacks of stuff. And then there were working men – crowds of 'em – digging up the ground. Using picks and shovels. Sweating hard.

'What are they doing?' I asked as we passed.

'Building a railway line,' Uncle Bert replied. 'Fine thing these new trains. Fine thing. It'll be the making of this town, mark my words.'

I saw rows of houses crammed together with no fields, no spaces round them – and I didn't like that. When we turned down a wider street, Uncle Bert called over his shoulder, 'This is the High Street.' He said lots more, but I didn't listen. I was busy looking at the buildings and shops on either side. There were inns and ale houses too. One of them was called Mother Red Cap and had a sign hanging over the door. The sign showed an old woman – warts and all – as scary as I'd ever seen.

'That's a queer name for a pub, Uncle,' I said.

'Named after a witch, so they say. Long gone now. Though folks have seen her ghost around the place.'

The thought of a ghost made me shiver and I didn't ask any more questions.

When we reached the farthest end of the High Street Uncle Bert finally stopped the cart outside a small shop. It was in terrible condition with a cracked and dusty window where two faded top hats were on display.

'Here we are,' said Aunt Maud, brushing the dust off her skirt. 'Mister Bagstone's gentlemen's hat shop. This is your new home.'

Eliza looked at me and rolled her eyes. 'This won't never be our home, will it, Sam?' she whispered and I shook my head. It looked like nobody's home to me. Just a miserable, worn-out place.

We all climbed out of the cart and went into the shop, which was dark and gloomy with cobwebs dripping from every cranny. There was a rough wooden counter and some shelves on the back wall displayed gentlemen's hats of all shapes and sizes. They were covered in a thick layer of dust so I reckoned they'd been there for years.

Alfie, who loved hats, pointed up to them. 'Can I try one on?' he whispered, and I winked at him and said, 'Later.'

Aunt Maud took us through a door into a room at the back where there was a bed squashed into the corner, a small table and a fireplace with a black pot hanging over the grate. It was nowhere near as grand as Uncle Bert had made out. 'You can eat in here but you'll sleep in the shop.'

Thinking she was going to feed us, we sat down. 'On your feet,' she shouted. 'Don't think you can be idle here. That cart needs emptying. Your uncle's tired after that long drive, so look to it.' We stood up. 'And when you've finished, you can give the shop a clean.'

We hurried outside and began to unload the cart.

Eliza was in a real temper. She wasn't used to being spoken to like that. Ma and Pa were strict but they never shouted at us. Now Alfie was snivelling.

'Cheer up,' I said. 'It'll be good having some of our old things around the place. They'll remind us of home.'

But I was wrong.

Uncle Bert pawed over our pots and pans as we carried them into the back room. 'These'll fetch a bob or two, missus,' he said to Aunt Maud. 'I'll take 'em down the market tomorrow.'

I was suddenly boiling with anger. He shouldn't sell 'em. They was ours by rights. I clenched my fists, wanting to punch the lights out of him. But I didn't. I marched outside to the cart and kicked the wheel instead.

The last things on the cart were Pa's books. 'I'll take one of 'em,' I whispered to Eliza. 'He'll never notice.' I chose *Oliver Twist* and pushed it under my jacket before I went back inside.

Aunt Maud had already found brushes and pieces of rag for us. 'Now get on and sweep the shop floor and dust the shelves,' she said.

20

We were tired, I can tell you, but while we managed to talk without our aunt and uncle hearing us, we looked around and I soon spotted a cupboard in the corner.

'It'll be just the place to hide Pa's book and the box,' said Eliza. It was so full of rubbish it was clear that nobody ever opened it.

'You're not to tell Aunt Maud or Uncle Bert,' I said to Alfie. 'Not anybody.'

'Cross my heart and hope to die,' he promised.

Later, when we'd finished the cleaning, Aunt Maud came and inspected it.

'Not perfect,' she said. 'But there's bread and cheese in the back room. Be thankful you'll have food in your bellies.'

We sat at the table, tired and covered in dust. The fire had been lit and Uncle Bert was snoring in his chair. Then from the shop a voice called, 'Evenin' all.' Seconds later, a man as big as a mountain poked his head round the door.

'How are yer, Missus B?' he said in a strange accent, though he looked pleasant enough. 'Are yer up for a pint at the Mother Red Cap, Bert?' he called across to Uncle Bert. 'Me and the lads will be goin' once we've cleaned ourselves up.'

'There's water in your bowl,' said Aunt Maud, not returning the smile. 'And there's a towel to dry yourself.'

'Ta, Missus B. It'll be nice to get rid of the filth, so it will.'

Uncle Bert sat up, suddenly wide awake. 'Give me five minutes and I'll join yer, Paddy.'

Aunt Maud told us later that Paddy was one of four Irish men who worked on the railway line and rented the room upstairs. This was why she and Uncle Bert slept in the back room.

'I don't like having them Irish workers in my house,' she said as Uncle Bert got out of his chair. 'They're a rough lot.'

'It's my house, missus,' Uncle Bert replied. 'They pays well, and I'll tell you this, when they finish building that railway, folks will come flocking from London on them trains. Before you know it, business will be booming and I'll be as rich as a lord.'

'I don't doubt it, husband,' said Aunt Maud. 'But do you have to drink with them workers? It don't seem right for a respectable businessman like you.'

'Stow it, woman,' Uncle Bert snapped. 'I'll drink with whoever I likes.' And he fetched his coat, put on his hat and went to spend the evening at the Mother Red Cap pub, which we'd passed in the High Street.

That night, Aunt Maud gave us a blanket each and we went to sleep in the shop. 'No fooling about,' she said. 'I know what children are like and I won't have it. You may be my dear sister's children, but I'll take a belt to you if I find you've been up to something.'

But we didn't care. As soon as she'd gone, Alfie whispered, 'Can I try on one o' them hats now?'

'Why not?' I grinned. 'We'll all try 'em, eh? It'll be good sport.'

And we did. Eliza looked best in a fine top hat, but Alfie chose one which was almost as battered as Uncle Bert's. He made us laugh cos it was so big that it fell down over his nose. After that, we played a game of how many top hats we could

22

stack in a pile. Alfie only managed three before they tumbled but Eliza was the champion. She made a pile of ten, which was more than I could do. It cheered us up no end.

'We'd better go to bed now,' I said, 'in case Aunt Maud comes in.'

'What bed?' said Eliza. 'You mean the floor, do yer?'

'Right. The floor. But as the hat champion, you get to choose which bit of the floor you'd like to sleep on.'

When we'd all settled down Alfie asked, 'Can we have a bit of *Oliver Twist*?' I agreed to read one chapter – the bit where Oliver asks for more – and then I said we should get some sleep.

We hadn't been sleeping long when the shop door burst open and we sat up to see five men stagger in singing some rude song at the top of their voices. Uncle Bert and the four Irish workmen leaned on the shop counter and when they looked over and saw us lying there, they roared with laughter and started singing even louder.

'What's going on?' Alfie asked, his face scrunched up in confusion. But before I could answer there was trouble. Aunt Maud, dressed in a long nightgown with a cap on her head, walked out from the back room.

'Mister Bagstone!' she shouted. 'What time do you call this?'

Uncle Bert giggled. 'Not late enough, wife.' And he roared as if he had made the funniest joke on earth.

Aunt Maud stormed over to him. 'You're drunk, husband. You have been wasting money in the ale house.'

Uncle Bert pulled himself up to his full height. 'No, madam. I have been doing business.'

'What *business* can you do in a pub? Tell me that.'

'Plenty,' he said, puffing out his chest, 'Tonight I found a job for that nephew of yours.' He swayed and pointed at me. 'That nephew what would eat us out of house and home, if I'm not mistaken. Ain't that good business, wife?'

And the next day I started work.

Five

Work

I was woken early before it was light.

'Get up,' said Uncle Bert prodding me with his foot. 'Paddy's waiting for yer.' And I sat up and rubbed my eyes, smelling the ale from last night on his breath.

Paddy, the Irish lodger we'd met yesterday, was leaning across the shop counter looking at me. 'Come on, lad,' he said. 'You're coming with me, working on the railway lines. You'll do all right, a fine boy like you.'

He seemed nice enough though we walked most of the way in silence, him rubbing his head and groaning after the drinking session at the Mother Red Cap. I was wondering what to expect – how would a boy like me make railway lines?

By the time we had reached the site on other side of town, men were already hard at work digging.

Paddy took me over to a man who was in charge and he handed me a shovel and a wooden wheelbarrow. 'He's a bit on the thin side, ain't he?' the foreman said, looking me up and down. 'But I'll give him a chance. He can work alongside you, Paddy. We'll see how he goes.'

Paddy picked up his own shovel and dropped it in the barrow. 'Follow me, lad,' he said. 'We're digging out the cutting this week.'

'What's that?'

'Making a flat path to run the track over. There's the cutting,' he said, pointing to a small hill. 'When we've finished digging out the earth, the train will run along it smooth as silk. That's the joy of it. No going uphill!'

Digging through a hill sounded like hard work. And it was. We shovelled soil into the barrow until my arms were aching. And when it was full, Paddy leaned on his shovel and said, 'See that horse and cart?' and pointed to the bottom of the hill. 'You take it over there, lad.'

The barrow was heavy but I managed to push it over to the cart and tip the soil into the back. Once it was full, the horse, who was called Captain, pulled it along a wooden track that ran up the side of the hill. It must have been really hard work for him. And dangerous too. On one trip that afternoon, the cart toppled over and I heard the horse cry out as it took him with it. Poor Captain lay there in pain, his legs flailing in the air, unable to get up.

All day I worked, digging and pushing the barrow backwards and forward until my muscles screamed and sweat ran down my back and soaked my shirt.

When the end of the day came at last, Paddy said, 'Good lad,' and patted me on the back. 'You're a hard worker, Sam, that's for sure. The foreman's impressed. He'll have work for you tomorrow, I'm certain.'

I got back to the shop, exhausted and thankful that the day was over.

'How was it?' asked Eliza as Alfie came running to greet me. 'Was it exciting, Sam?' he asked, flinging his arms round my knees. 'We've been washing the floor.'

Before I could tell them anything, Aunt Maud came out of the back room. 'There's a bucket of water in the back yard,' she said. 'Wash the dirt off your face before your uncle gets back.'

I'd cleaned myself up and gone back inside by the time Uncle Bert walked in.

'Worked hard, did yer, lad? Didn't go showing me up, did yer?' he said, wagging his finger. 'I'll expect to see some money by the end of the week.'

But he wasn't interested in a reply. He turned away, eager to tell Aunt Maud what he had been doing.

'I done a good deal,' he told her. 'Found work for them young uns right on our doorstep too. Do you doubt I'm a fine businessman, Missus Bagstone?'

'None better, husband.'

I kept quiet but crossed my fingers, hoping they wouldn't have to work as hard I had that day.

It turned out that Eliza and Alfie were to work with the undertaker next door who went by the name of Mister Dewsnap. That name had made us laugh when we'd arrived in Camden and we'd seen him standing outside his shop.

'That's a perfect name for him, ain't it?' Eliza had laughed as she pointed to the sign above the shop. 'Look, that dewdrop's quivering on the end of his great pointed nose! It's just waiting to drip.'

But it turned out that working for Mister Dewsnap was no laughing matter.

While I was digging the railway tracks, Alfie had to help make coffins in the yard at the back of the undertaker's shop. He held nails and passed them to Mister Dewsnap who was a miserable man and spoke very little so that the nipper felt lonely. Some days, the undertaker would set out with an empty coffin on his cart – the one Uncle Bert had borrowed to bring us to Camden.

'I've got to sit next to the coffin,' Alfie told me. 'I don't like it, Sam. He puts a dead body in it and I've got to make sure it don't fall off. But them bodies stink, they do.'

Every night, he cried a lot. I felt real sorry for him. He was only a nipper.

Eliza fared no better. She worked with Missus Dewsnap, who was as gloomy as her husband, and her job was gruesome.

'I can't tell you how bad it is, Sam,' she said. 'I've got to help the undertaker's wife to wash the bodies and dress them in white shrouds.'

'What are shrouds?'

'Sort of dresses for dead people,' she explained. 'And – worse than that – I have to help lift them bodies into the coffins and she makes me put the lids on. "Do it quick, girl," she says. "Keep the flies out." Oh, lawks, Sam. I can't bear it! I kept thinking them corpses will sit up.'

My work made my muscles ache but at least I slept well at night.

As the weeks passed, I tried to cheer them up by reading from Pa's book before we went to sleep.

'But don't read that bit where Oliver works for the undertaker,' said Eliza.

'No!' Alfie agreed. 'Not that bit. Tell us about the Artful Dodger.'

When I'd finished, Eliza always sang 'Twinkle Twinkle Little Star'. Ma used to sing it when Alfie couldn't sleep. He loved that song and he'd soon close his eyes and drift off.

Most nights, they had bad dreams about ghosts and things jumping out of coffins and chasing them. It was really bad, no matter what happy things we talked about before we went to sleep one of them would wake, screaming.

'I can't stand it no more, Sam,' Eliza would say. 'I want to go home.'

We talked about running away, but we never did. We were skint, see. Even though we worked six days a week from early in the morning till late at night, we never saw so much as a farthing. Whatever money we earned, Uncle Bert took it at the end of the week and spent it down at Mother Red Cap's.

'I'm off to do important business,' he'd say. But we all knew where he was going. He was joining Paddy and the others who rented the upstairs room. When he came home it was very late and he'd stumble through the shop while we were trying to sleep. Once he was in the back room, there'd be a terrible shindy.

'You've been drinking again!' Aunt Maud would yell.

'Don't look so sour, Missus. Them young uns are bringing in extra money.'

'And you're spending it.'

'Stow it, woman. It's a man's right to enjoy himself once in a while.'

But the 'once in a while' turned into every night.

The funny thing was – the crosser Aunt Maud got with Uncle Bert, the kinder she was to us. She made sure we had food every day and she'd sometimes give us a treat – like an extra helping of rice pudding – when Uncle Bert wasn't looking. She was never going to be the same as our Ma, but we grew quite fond of her in our own way.

One morning on our way to work, Paddy said, 'That uncle of yours is very free with his money, so he is. Some gamblers have been showing him a few cards games in the pub and I'm thinking he'd like to be a gambling man himself.'

I'd grown to like Paddy, and I could see that he was right.

One night, Uncle Bert came home in a high old mood. There was the usual quarrel and I heard him say, 'See here, missus. These are my winnings. It seems I've got a gift for the card games. I'll make some good money.' And she shouted back, 'That's gambling! You've got responsibilities now, husband, think of those children!'

And the truth was Uncle Bert was a real stupe. A five-year-old kid would know you couldn't make easy money from gambling. But he didn't. As the weeks passed, he used the money we earned to put bigger bets on the cards and thought he could go on winning for ever. But he soon began to lose. The gamblers in the Mother Red Cap probably cheated him. I think he was easily tricked.

Every night, he and Aunt Maud quarrelled and they'd be yelling and shouting till all hours.

'Can't you see that things will get better, woman?' he'd say. 'I'll win tomorrow and make my fortune. So stop yer blathering.'

Day after day, he lost at the cards. Our aunt looked grimmer than ever and worry lines appeared on her forehead. Nothing she said made any difference and soon there was hardly any money for food. Uncle Bert sold whatever he could – vases, Aunt Maud's clock and even her best clothes. Everything went.

By the end of that summer, he was in debt and there was nothing for it but to sell the shop. The undertaker, Mister Dewsnap, bought it for less that it was worth (which wasn't much).

The money from the sale of the shop made Uncle Bert very happy. He held the large bundle of notes in his hand and said, 'Now my luck will change, missus. This will make my fortune, just you see.'

Aunt Maud begged him not to go but he set off that evening for the Mother Red Cap with the money in his pocket.

'Ruined! What will become of us all?' she sobbed, and she fell to her knees as he walked out of the door. Eliza tried to quiet her, telling her we'd find a way, but there was no consoling her.

That night Uncle Bert staggered home from the pub, roaring drunk. He didn't make it as far as the back room but collapsed on the floor of the shop. When Aunt Maud heard the noise, she came running out while we came from the other side of the counter to see if we could help.

'My luck has flown!' Uncle Bert moaned as we all tried to lift him. 'I did my best, but luck was not with me.'

Knowing that all was lost, Aunt Maud covered her face with her hands and burst into tears. Eliza, Alfie and me looked at each other. She was no angel, but she'd tried to be kind to us and we felt sorry for her being married to someone as stupid as Uncle Bert. Now she had no money and nowhere to live. And neither did we.

'Don't get yourself into a bother, wife,' said Uncle Bert struggling to stand up. 'Camden isn't much of a place, anyhow. I know somewhere better. We can live there like royalty for next to nothing. There's money to be made and I'll be rich in no time.'

With bloodshot eyes, he turned to look at us. 'I'll soon be rich, won't I, young uns?' And he winked at us, thinking we'd believe him. But, of course, we didn't. 'Mark my words,' he said, 'we'll have a fine life.'

Early the next morning, we all left Camden for good. I hid Pa's book in my jacket while Eliza wrapped the silver box in her shawl. Then we set off. Uncle Bert told us we were headed to a place called Devil's Acre. The name sent a shudder down my spine, and true enough, it turned out to be the dirtiest, scariest part of London, full of dippers and cut-throats. But I'd promised Pa I'd look after the young uns. And nobody would touch 'em while I was around, I'd make sure of it. I could whack a real punch when I needed to.

Devil's Acre was right behind Westminster Abbey. It was odd when you think about it. There was the abbey, full of priests kneeling and praying and lighting candles, while only a few yards away, hungry families were jammed together in lodging houses with thieves and murderers for neighbours.

This was the place where we went to live.

Six

Devil's Acre

When we lived in Camden I thought that was a busy town, I soon discovered that it was nothing compared with London.

There the streets were the busiest in the world; they were so crowded that it was hard to walk along the pavement without bumping into somebody. And the roads were so thick with horse dung and mud that there were young uns carrying brushes and shouting, 'Sweep your crossing, lady. Only a penny.' That way, people who could afford it could walk from one side to the other without getting their boots dirty.

'Cripes!' I said to Eliza as we headed into the city. 'Have you ever seen such a crush?'

She shook her head. 'No, I ain't. And it smells worse than a farmyard, don't it?'

'Look at them horses!' yelled Alfie as a carriage whizzed past carrying three toffs. Their driver sat up front, dressed smart as you please, wagging his whip in the air just so we'd notice him. 'Can we have a ride, mister?' Alfie called but they took no notice.

The roads in London were long and straight and lined with

houses – row after row of them, there were. Hundreds of houses and shops. And buildings as big as churches – that's the truth.

We'd been walking all morning and part of the afternoon when we came upon a park. Real splendiferous sight it was. A bit like the country but the grass was very short and there weren't no cows nor hens. There was a big lake, though, with ducks and swans and families were strolling around, chatting.

'Are we going to live here?' asked Alfie. 'It's good. We could play here, couldn't we, Sam?'

Aunt Maud, who looked very sad and had hardly said a word all the way, shook her head. 'This is St James's Park, Alfie. We won't be living here.'

I saw Alfie's face drop. 'We could stop here and have a play, couldn't we, Aunt Maud?' I asked.

Uncle Bert seemed grateful for the rest and sat down straight away, so Aunt Maud nodded. Alfie grinned and pulled off his boots. Then he ran down to the lake side, dipping his toes in the water and splashing and flapping his arms at the ducks.

'Lawks!' said Eliza looking about. 'It's bigger than a farmer's field. What's it doing in the middle of London?'

'Dunno,' I said. I flopped down onto the grass, glad of the rest and sat there wondering what was going to happen to us now.

After a while, Uncle Bert got to his feet. 'Best get moving before it gets dark,' he said, patting his top hat firmly on his head. 'Not far now and I'll find us a place for the night.'

We left the park and crossed over a road called Birdcage Walk. That's where everything changed. No more grass. No more grand houses. We were suddenly plunged into gloomy streets which led to narrow alleys and crooked passageways. There were no fine buildings here, only crumbling houses jammed together so tight that if you leaned out of a bedroom window, you could shake hands with your neighbour in the house opposite. True! Those buildings were so close that, even on a sunny day, the light wouldn't reach as far as the ground.

Alfie was frightened. 'It's dark, Sam. I don't like it. I don't.' So I picked him up and carried him the rest of the way, Eliza close at our side.

'Why do we have to come here, Sam?' she whispered, not wanting Uncle Bert to hear. 'I'm scared somebody will jump out and snatch me.'

No wonder they were frightened. I was scared myself, though I tried not to show it – me being thirteen and grown up.

We moved into a crumbling lodging house in the narrowest and dirtiest alley of all. I don't know how many families lived in that house. I never did find out.

There was a rickety staircase up to the top floor where kids, half-naked, played and jumped about at all hours of the day. They'd call to us, as we climbed the stairs, 'Hey, gingerheads! Got any money?'

The room we rented was on the third floor. It was small – hardly big enough for the five of us – with a window, partly covered in brown paper to keep out the wind. There was a fireplace, a bed and a small table that wobbled. There wasn't anything else. There was no space.

'This is just temporary, like,' said Uncle Bert as he parked himself on the bed and lit his pipe. 'Once I've made a bit of money, we'll be out of here and living somewhere grand, you'll see. But you kids'll have to knuckle down. Get to work, eh? Fine kids like you. Should be no trouble.'

We had heard it all before. I didn't believe things would get better, and I could tell Aunt Maud didn't, either – she looked thin and miserable and very, very sad. But she was fond of us in her own way, especially Alfie – only he could make her smile.

I wasn't long before I learned how poor people lived in that part of London, packed together in the rooms of lodging houses, sharing one stinking outhouse in the yard with dozens of others. And when they couldn't be bothered to go down to the yard, they emptied their chamber pots out of the window. The smell of those alleys was horrible.

No wonder they called it Devil's Acre.

During the time we lived there we found work wherever we could – which wasn't as easy as you'd think. Folks didn't have a jammy life there. Most of 'em were trying to make a living, but finding work was hard, see.

A lot of people went thieving. Some of the kids in Devil's Acre were dippers – they took handkerchiefs and wallets and stuff – but they often got nicked and dragged in front of the beak. But even when we couldn't get work, we never stole nothing. Ma and Pa would have been furious if we had. We'd been brought up honest, see.

Most jobs for the likes of me paid real bad. At first I was a crossing sweeper. All day I worked in the cold and rain, cleaning muck and rubbish off the streets for just a few pennies. Soon after that, I got work carrying hot potatoes from the baker's oven to a seller on the Strand. They paid me four pence a day. But it didn't last long. I was sent away when another lad came and did the same job for tuppence. And when I couldn't find work after that, I went and waded in the mud by the river, looking for bits to sell.

Uncle Bert got some work in Covent Garden, sweeping up and helping the porters. He'd come home in the afternoon with few rotting vegetables and we'd go out and try to sell 'em. But that didn't last long, either.

We did all sorts of things to earn a few pennies. But there was one thing Aunt Maud wouldn't allow and that was sending Alfie sweeping chimneys. That was the worst job. We'd heard terrible tales from kids in Devil's Acre. How little uns were sent up narrow chimneys and never came down again.

But our uncle and aunt had some terrible rows about it. 'I know a fella,' Bert said one time. 'He's short of a boy and he'll pay well. Our Alfie's just the right size.'

'No, no, no,' said Aunt Maud. 'It's dangerous. He'll get stuck, he will.'

'But he'll earn a good wage,' Uncle Bert insisted. 'And if he gets stuck and dies, this fella said he'd pay us extra.'

The thought of Alfie up a chimney made my belly churn.

But Aunt Maud wasn't having any of it and threw up her hands in horror. 'No. Most definitely, no!' And that was an end to it. Uncle Bert left in a real grump and we all put our arms round Aunt Maud and hugged her to show her how grateful we were.

It was November. We had been in Devil's Acre for over a year and winter was coming on. Uncle Bert hadn't become rich like he said he would – but we weren't surprised. There was barely enough money to pay the rent and buy food. We were as thin as sticks and our skin had turned a grey colour through want of a proper wash.

Eliza was twelve by then and Alfie was six. Our clothes were worn thin and were much too small. Aunt Maud cut down a pair of Uncle Bert's trousers for me and I gave mine to Alfie. Sometimes, I'd see myself reflected in a shop window, looking like a walking scarecrow, and I was glad Ma and Pa couldn't see us like that. Boots were the worst thing. When the nipper's feet got too big he wailed, 'My feet hurts bad, Sam.' So I cut holes in the toes to make them more comfy, but it wasn't long before the soles wore away. We were all the same and soon we went barefoot – which wasn't as bad as you think. Our feet got tough as old leather and we hardly noticed.

That was how life was in Devil's Acre. Like hundreds of families, we lived as best we could.

Seven

Eliza sings

One day, Alfie and me got back home after working by the river to find Eliza and Uncle Bert having a right shindy. It was surprising cos I'd always thought Eliza was quite scared of him.

'What's all this about?' I asked, walking into the room.

Uncle Bert sniffed and waved his hand at Eliza. 'You ask *her* what it's about. Go on, girl. You tell him. Tell him who's given up her job after only two days. *Two days, I ask you!* That job would have kept this family in good wholesome food. You tell him whose fault it is if we all starve to death!' Then he began to pace up and down – as much as the tiny room would allow.

And all this time, Aunt Maud was up in the corner clutching her apron and not saying a word.

Eliza turned to me and Alfie. 'The factory caught fire and Mister Stoker got burned in the drying room. That's what happened.'

'Which bit of him got burned?' asked Alfie.

'All of him,' Eliza replied. 'Burned dead, he was.'

'Like toast? Did you see him?'

'No I didn't, Alfie. I came home,' Eliza snapped. 'It's a

wonder nobody else was hurt. That match factory's a death trap, if you ask me.' She put on her stubborn face. 'And I ain't never working there again.'

'See!' yelled Uncle Bert, wagging his finger at Eliza. 'After all I've done for her and she won't work – young and healthy as she is – while her poor old aunt and uncle have all the troubles of old age.'

'I won't be healthy for long if I works in one of them places,' Eliza shouted. 'My teeth will fall out and my face will swell up like an apple. I've seen it. Them girls look horrible, they do. I'll go begging on the streets before I make them matches.'

'Fair enough,' I said, wanting all the shouting to be over with. 'That seems a good reason for giving up the job, don't it, Auntie?'

Aunt Maud nodded in agreement. And realising that he'd lost the argument, Uncle Bert stormed out of the room shouting that, seeing as no one else was bringing any money home, he'd go looking for work. We didn't believe him, of course. He hadn't earned as much as a penny in months.

Aunt Maud put her arm round Eliza. 'Never you mind, girl. You were quite right. A match factory's no place for you.'

'We'll find Eliza something else, don't worry,' I said. 'Got anything to eat, Auntie? I'm starving.' She pointed to the shelf where half a loaf was waiting patiently to be eaten. I broke it into four pieces and we sat on the bed and ate it.

'Find anything by the river, did yer?' asked Aunt Maud.

I handed her a rusty kettle I'd filled with two lumps of coal, some pieces of wood and a bit of metal.

'There weren't much,' I said as she peered inside. 'But it's better than nothing, eh?'

'We found a sack under the bridge,' said Alfie. 'We thought it was treasure and we'd be rich. But it was a dead cat.'

'Ugh!' said Eliza. 'That's horrible.'

'No it wasn't. He was a nice cat,' said Alfie, who loved animals. 'But Sam said you can't sell dead cats.'

Eliza started singing, 'Ding Dong Bell, Pussy's in the Well' to try and cheer him up, but it only set him off crying.

Aunt Maud, put her arm round Alfie to quieten him and then she turned to Eliza with a thoughtful look on her face. 'You've got a real pretty voice, girl, just like your ma's. When I've passed the beer shop down Old Pye Street, I've heard singers no better than you.'

'What do you mean, Aunt?' I asked. 'Do they have entertainers?'

'They do, I believe.'

'And will they pay?'

Aunt Maud laughed. 'The singers go round with a hat. That's what usually happens, I think.'

I looked at Eliza. 'How about it?' I said. 'Think you could sing in the beer shop and make a bob or two?'

'Why not?' she said.

It sounded like a good idea to me. Eliza could sing as sweet as a lark and Alfie could dance a bit – sailor's hornpipe, that kind of thing. I could go round with a cap to collect the money and then I'd be there to look after the two of 'em. What's the harm? What could go wrong?

'What about you, Alfie? Will you do a dance?'

'I can dance,' he said and jumped up to show us a sailor's hornpipe. But as he began he let out a squeal. 'Ouch! Me foot hurts.'

Eliza, bent down to take a look. 'You've cut it, Alfie. Did you step on some broken glass down by the river?' She checked there weren't anything stuck in the cut and then lifted her skirt and tore a strip of cloth from her petticoat. 'This should do the trick,' she said and gave a good gob of spittle onto the cloth, wiped Alfie's foot clean and tied the cloth round it. Grand job!

'Does that feel comfy?' she asked. 'Will you be able to dance all right?'

Alfie grinned and gave us a fine demonstration.

We set off to the beer shop in a high old mood, hoping to make our fortune. 'Can we sing a song for your customers, mister?' I asked the landlord.

He shook his head. 'They're a rough lot,' he said, nodding towards a group of costermongers. 'This is no place for young uns.'

'Go on, mister,' Eliza pleaded. 'Give us a chance.'

He looked doubtful but, what with Eliza's bright smile and her red curls, and Alfie's skinny face he took pity on us. 'Go on, then,' he said and Eliza grinned and thanked him.

The costermongers were big men in corduroy trousers and flat caps. They must've finished their day's work, pushing carts of fish or vegetables round the streets and come to the beer shop for a pint of ale and some company. Some were sitting at small tables playing cribbage, holding cards in one hand and a drink in the other.

'Good evening, gents!' Eliza called out bold as you like, standing in the middle of the room. But the costermongers were too busy to pay her any attention.

So she started to sing. The song was 'The Soldier's Dream', what Ma had taught us, and the costermongers must have liked it because they put their cards down and listened. When she finished they cheered and that was when the nipper stepped up onto a table and did his little dance, which made them laugh. They clapped when he'd finished and then it was my time to walk round with my cap to collect the pennies. The costermongers were a noisy lot but they were free with their money and, altogether, they dropped one shilling and tuppence in my cap. Enough to buy us a good supper. Jammy, eh?

'I'll sing another one,' said Eliza. 'See if we can make any more.'

Just as she was about to start again, the door opened and two men stepped inside. They were roughly dressed with mufflers round their necks and caps pulled down over their foreheads. I must admit, I didn't like the look of them and wondered if we should take what we'd got and get out of there.

'Evening, gents,' called the landlord. 'Two new faces, I see. Will you take some ale?'

The strangers bought a small glass of beer each and went to sit by two of the costermongers.

'Will you join us in a game of cribbage?' asked one of them. He must have been thinking it was a chance to make easy money from the newcomers.

The strangers nodded and cards were placed on the table while the other costermongers gathered round to watch. I thought it was best to wait until the game was over before Eliza sang again. But after three games, the strangers had lost every penny they had.

'Them cards is marked,' they yelled, springing to their feet. 'Cheats! That's what you are!'

The costermongers slowly stood up and clenched their fists. 'Calling us cheats, are you?' said one. 'Nobody calls us that.'

It seemed to me that there was nothing the costermongers enjoyed so much as a good fight. Soon fists were flying, tables were overturned, beer was spilled, noses were bashed and bleeding as they all joined in.

The landlord looked across at us. 'I told you, didn't I?' he shouted. 'Now get out quick before you get hurt and don't come back.'

We rushed towards the door but I tripped and fell. Lawks! The money spilled from my cap and scattered across the floor. I groaned, angry with myself for being so clumsy.

'Come on, Sam,' Eliza said, grabbing my arm to help me up. 'Let's get out of here.' But I shook it free.

'You and Alfie wait outside,' I said. 'I'm not leaving without that money.'

The coins had rolled across the crowded room. I scrabbled after them, crawling over the floor, through the beefy legs of the costermongers. Several times their great boots trampled on my fingers. 'Oi, leave off!' I shouted but it weren't no use. They were all yelling and balling too much to hear. Anyway, I managed to get most of the coins except for three pennies which fell between the cracks in the floorboards.

'You all right, Sam?' Eliza asked, once I was outside.

I nodded, gasping for breath and pressing my hands between my legs, waiting for the pain to go away.

'I got the money,' I said. 'The sooner we give it to Aunt Maud, the sooner we'll have food in our bellies. Come on.'

We hurried down Old Pye Street and through the alleyways till we reached the front door of the lodging house and it was then that we heard Aunt Maud's voice, screeching and hollering.

I looked up at the window.

'I think Uncle Bert's back.'

Eight

Uncle Bert's troubles

After months of living with Aunt Maud and Uncle Bert, we were used to their arguments, especially about money. It didn't bother us any more – not even Alfie.

So we climbed the stairs to our room and walked in as if things were normal. Uncle Bert was over by the window, his battered top hat at an awkward angle and his face flushed the colour of beetroot. This was a sure sign he had stopped for a beer or two on the way home.

'Tell me the truth, Mister Bagstone!' Aunt Maud shrieked, not even noticing that we'd come in. 'Where've you been till now?'

'Stop your griping, woman,' he said. 'One of the porters' carts broke and I helped him mend it. He paid me a shilling, he did.'

Maud held out her hand. 'Give it here. I want to see it.'

Uncle Bert shook his head. 'Ain't a man entitled to a bit of pleasure after a hard day's work?'

'Where's the shilling? Drunk it away at the pub, have yer?'

'Not so, missus,' he said straightening his hat. 'I invested it, I did.'

I groaned.

Maud's eyes grew big as door knobs. 'Invested it? How?'

'I tell you I was *this close* to having a fortune,' he said, holding his thumb and forefinger together. 'I was very nearly rich, I was. Very, very rich.' Then he looked away and sighed. 'But my luck was out.'

'Luck? What luck? You ain't had any luck for years.'

'You don't understand nothin' about business, missus.' He slumped on the edge of the bed. 'There was some rat baiting out in the yard of the One Tun.'

Alfie looked alarmed at the thought of rat baiting and I put my arm round the nipper, hoping the argument would soon be over.

'I was near to winning fifty pounds, missus. Fifty pounds, do you hear? A fortune! I was planning to rent us some fine rooms, with a maid and all. I was going to buy us fresh cooked meat and a bed with a feather mattress.'

Aunt Maud narrowed her eyes, not believing a word. 'Very nice, I'm sure. So what happened?'

Uncle Bert shrugged. 'I'd already won five pounds, see. Things were going well. Then some cove told me about a new dog what would kill thirty rats for certain.' Alfie shuddered and I pulled him close. 'Good tip, it was. So I went and asked the landlord to lend me ten pounds so I could place a big bet and win a fortune.'

'You did what?' yelled Aunt Maud. 'You asked that old devil Beddows to lend you money?' She swiped him across the shoulder, sending him tumbling to the floor. 'You gambled with money you didn't have?' By then her face had turned red and I was expecting her to explode any minute.

'I was tricked!' said Uncle Bert as he got to his feet. 'That dog was useless. Only got three rats. The man was a liar.'

'Of course he was a liar!' Aunt Maud screeched. 'He was in league with Beddows, weren't he? Any fool would know that!' She raised her hand to swipe him again.

'Now, wife,' Bert protested and ducked out of the way.

By then she was in a real mood. She picked up a lump of coal and sent it fizzing towards him, but he dodged to one side so that it went crashing through the window pane and down into the alley.

'Fetch that coal back, Sam,' she said, 'I didn't intend to miss your uncle like that. Can't go wasting coal.'

We all ran down the stairs, glad to be out of the way. The coal was in the alley broken in pieces but we did our best to pick them up. By the time we got back, the room was quiet except for Aunt Maud who was sniffing and snivelling, holding a handkerchief to her face.

'You had a busy day, Uncle?' I asked pretending I hadn't overheard the quarrel.

Uncle Bert straightened his back and tugged the brim of his ancient top hat in the manner of a gentleman. 'Very busy, my boy,' he said, and coughed in a nervous sort of way. 'And now, I am sorry to say, I have some bad news.'

'What's that?' I asked, wondering how things could be any worse.

He coughed again. 'It has become necessary for me to move on.'

'Where to this time?' Eliza asked.

'Away from here,' Bert replied. 'I was once a man of fine reputation with a good income and a roof over my head. But things were against me and...' He waved his hand dramatically round the cramped, shabby room. 'I am brought low. Now I must leave this hovel before some unsavoury characters come to demand money from me.'

At these words, Aunt Maud set up such a howling that it could be heard for a mile or more. 'Oh, Mister Bagstone. I'm too old for movin', I tell you.' And she sank to the floor, covering her face with her apron.

Poor Aunt Maud sobbed and wailed. 'What shall we do?' she said over and over while her husband stared out of the window.

When she calmed herself, she wiped her face and got to her feet. 'Well then,' she said, smiling at us and smoothing her tattered old apron. 'We'll have to make the best of it, shan't we? Come on, we'll get our things together and be on our way.'

But Bert shook his head. 'No, missus,' he said. 'Them young uns are your sister's. I never wanted 'em in the first place. They ain't coming with us this time.'

I couldn't believe it. Was he was leaving us in Devil's Acre? Alfie started sobbing and Eliza put her arms round him, while Aunt Maud stood and stared at Uncle Bert, her mouth open with the shock of it.

'Not coming? What can you mean, husband? I promised my sister on her deathbed that I'd look after her children, I did.'

Uncle Bert lifted his chin in defiance before tapping his hat and attempting to button up his jacket. 'It ain't no use, missus. Them children's too big. They keep on growin'. Eatin' and growin', that's all they do. Anyhow, it was your promise. I can't afford to feed 'em no more.'

'So, what'll happen to us, Uncle?' Eliza asked.

'He's leaving us, that's what,' I said, clenching my fists wishing I could thump the selfish old goat. 'He won't care about us, will he?'

'Watch your temper, boy,' snapped Uncle Bert. 'No need to be ill-mannered.' He adjusted his hat and said, 'I have come up with an excellent plan for you.'

'Oh indeed, Mister Bagstone,' said Aunt Maud. 'And what would that be?'

'Listen, woman,' he snapped. 'Their father might have run off to foreign parts, but we don't have to look after his children for ever, do we?'

'Are we going to abandon them to starve?' she yelled.

Uncle Bert wagged his finger. 'They've got a rich grandfather, ain't they? I did think we could get some money out of him for myself, but he won't have anything to do with you and your sister. It would be a waste of time.'

I thought he was talking rubbish. I'd never heard of a grandfather. But Aunt Maud seemed to know what he was on about.

'So what about their grandfather?' she said.

'Well, why shouldn't he have 'em? He's rich, ain't he?'

Aunt Maud nodded.

'Then let 'em go to him, I say.'

Aunt Maud chewed on her fingernail while she thought about it. 'You might have a point, Mister Bagstone. He could look after them very nicely.'

'The lad's nearly fifteen now,' said Uncle Bert, pointing at me. 'He's man enough to go and see his grandfather. He can take the other two with him. Can't he do that?'

I didn't know whether to feel angry or excited. On one hand, he was leaving us on our own. But on the other, we'd found out we had a grandfather. That was good wasn't it? Our grandfather might look after us properly. So what had we got to lose? Nothing was worse than living with Uncle Bert in Devil's Acre. And we had family we never knew about – a rich family! It was exciting! Really! I could hardly believe it!

'I can do that,' I said. 'Where does our grandfather live?'

'In the country,' Aunt Maud explained. 'He's got a fine house, I believe.'

Eliza pushed her hair away from her face. 'But what if he doesn't want us? We've never met him.'

'He'll see you're right, I'm sure,' said Aunt Maud giving her a hug. 'Only somebody with a heart of stone would turn you away.' She glared at her husband. 'You're better off without us, I'm sure your mother wouldn't want me to drag you down with us. This is for the best, though it breaks my heart to leave you.'

With that, she fetched a piece of paper, a quill pen and a bottle of ink off the shelf by the fireplace.

'I'll write to the old gentleman,' she said.

Eliza looked surprised and said, 'Ma didn't know how to write.'

Aunt Maud smiled a sad sort of smile. 'I know,' she replied. 'Your mother never went to the dame school, child.' And she patted her hand before picking up the quill and starting the letter. 'I'll ask him to take you in, but you should know, he ain't spoken to his son since he married my sister,' she said shaking her head. 'Shameful! He cut your pa off without a penny.

All of a sudden, as she said those words, there were butterflies in my belly. If our grandfather could turn his son away, surely he wouldn't want to see his grandchildren, would he? I could tell Eliza was worried. But what choice did we have? More than anything, we wanted Pa to come for us, but we couldn't just wait around for that to happen. I'd never said it to the young uns, but I feared we'd never see him again. A grandfather, even one we didn't know, had to be our best chance now.

When Aunt Maud had finished the letter, she folded the paper and wrote the name and address on the front. 'You give him that when you see him, Sam,' she said as she handed it to me and I put it in my pocket.

All this time, Uncle Bert had been looking out of the window as nervous as a cat in a dog kennel, and suddenly he yelled, 'Cripes! They're here already, missus. I can see 'em. Beddows's men are in the alley! They're nearly here! They've come for the money! Don't just stand there, woman.'

As we heard footsteps pounding up the stairs, Uncle Bert climbed unsteadily out of the window, knocking off his hat as he leaned forward to grab the drainpipe. 'If you don't want to see me battered to death, you'd better come quick,' he howled, before leaping off the sill and slithering towards the ground at an alarming speed. I never knew he could move that fast.

Hardly knowing which way to turn, Aunt Maud grabbed her bonnet and pulled it on. 'I'm sorry,' she said. 'I did as best I could for you. But I've got to go. Take care of each other, especially my little Alfie. Promise you'll find your grandpa.' Gathering her skirt in her hand, she struggled up onto the window ledge then, shrieking and hollering, she slid down the drainpipe.

Nine

Gone

I quickly put the new letter in the silver box with Pa's letters and pushed it under the bed where we kept it hidden. If Uncle Bert had seen that box, he would have sold it in the blink of an eye.

'What do we do now?' asked Eliza.

Before I could answer, two thugs burst into the room. They were a bloodcurdling pair with jaws as broad as shovels and fists the size of cabbages. I wondered how on earth I could protect our Eliza and the nipper from these two.

'Where's the old man?' the first one growled at me. 'Tell me or else!'

I was shaking like a leaf in the wind, though I tried not to show it. Alfie was cowering in the corner and Eliza was sitting on the bed, covering her face with her hands.

'If you're looking for our uncle,' I said, pretending to be calm, 'he ain't here, mister. He's gone to find work.'

'Looking for work, is he?' sneered the second man, who had cheeks scarred from one side to the other and a nose knocked half across his face. 'You're telling lies, lad. Your uncle's only just left the One Tun and he's run off without paying his dues. Owes Mister Beddows a lot of money, he does. And if he's hiding we'll find him, won't we, Arthur?'

The thug called Arthur grinned, showing a row of yellow, rotting teeth. 'We'll find him, Charlie,' he said, grabbing hold of the straw mattress and tipping Eliza onto the floor where she lay in a heap between the wooden bed frame and the wall. She didn't scream or yell or nothing. She just lay there.

'You can see our uncle ain't here!' I said. 'There ain't nowhere to hide.'

The man called Arthur was on his knees reaching under the bed frame. 'Look what I found,' he said.

Charlie laughed. 'Found Bert Bagstone down there, have yer?'

'Nah, but I found this,' Arthur said and waved the silver box in the air. My stomach sank. I'd thought it was safe there.

But when Charlie looked at Ma's box, he seemed disappointed. 'What's that?'

'It's just an old box,' I said. 'We had it when we was kids.'

Arthur narrowed his eyes, suspicious like. 'Then why did you hide it? Somethink inside, is there?'

'No. Nothing!' I said. 'We keep it cos our ma gave it us. She's dead, see.'

Arthur didn't care. He glanced across at this mate. 'What do you reckon, Charlie? The lad looks like a thief to me. Open the box and see if he's hiding some fancy jewellery.'

Charlie opened the box and looked inside. 'Just rubbish,' he said taking out the letters.

'Are those your ma's?' asked Arthur, and when I nodded, he

said, 'You're right, Charlie – just rubbish in an old tin box.' Charlie sneered and spat on the letters before he stuffed them back inside the box. Then he threw it on the floor.

Alfie stood up and I could see he was angry at the way they'd treated Ma's box.

'It ain't rubbish! It ain't!' he shouted and stepped towards them. 'It's silver, that is.'

The bullies laughed and knocked Alfie to the floor, leaving him sobbing. I rushed over to him, trying to grab the box at the same time.

But Arthur snatched it up. 'Let's have another look at that box,' he said turning it over in his grubby hands. 'Well, I'm blowed!' he said, staring at the box. 'It's silver, all right! And there was I thinking it was just a bit of old tin.' He looked looked up at Charlie. 'It needs cleaning up, that's all. But Beddows will be well pleased when we hand this over. He'll be very pleased indeed.'

Charlie grinned and punched him on the shoulder. 'We'll be in the money! Tomorrow, we could treat ourselves to a day off. A nice balcony seat at the Vic, eh, Arthur?'

'Nah! Don't fancy a play.'

'They say there's a murder in it.'

'Nah! Let's go over to Battersea in the morning – have a bit of pigeon shooting at the Red House.'

While they were deciding how to spend their reward, they were looking round for anything else they could sell. They took the old kettle, a wooden stool and Aunt Maud's sack but they left a tin plate, two mugs and *Oliver Twist*.

As they turned to leave, Arthur pointed a threatening finger at us which scared us half to death. 'You tell your uncle we'll be looking for him. Tell him that!' And the thugs walked out of the door, taking the silver box and the letters with them.

Ten

Missus Abdale's meat pies

Beddows's men had taken Ma's box and in it was the letter with Grandpa's address. I hadn't even read it. I didn't know where he lived. Where could we go now?

Alfie was still crying. 'I'm sorry, Sam. Sorry I told them about the box.'

There was no point in being cross and I didn't want to show him how worried I was, so I said, 'Don't worry, nipper. It's all right, ain't it, Eliza?'

But Eliza didn't utter a word. She hadn't since the thugs arrived, I realised. Even as she struggled to stand up, she didn't speak. But once she was on her feet, she gave us both a surprise.

She opened her mouth wide and spat out eleven pennies onto the mattress.

'Lawks!' I said.

'Cripes!' said Alfie

She groaned. '*Ugggggh!*' and wiped her lips with the back of her hand. 'Them coins taste something horrible.'

Alfie grinned. 'Is that why you kept quiet, Eliza? I thought you was scared.'

'Nah! Not me. But I weren't going to let them bullies take our money as well. If I'd said anything, they'd have known straight away there was something in my mouth.'

'That's clever, that is,' said Alfie. 'Can we go and buy a pie now? Me belly's begging for something to eat.'

I wanted to talk to Eliza about losing our Grandpa's address. I was more bothered about that than the box, and I expect she was worried about it too. But I didn't want to upset Alfie, see. So I thought it could wait until later when he was asleep.

'Course we can get a pie,' I said as I lifted the mattress back onto the bed. 'We're rich, ain't we? We'll have a pie each.'

But Alfie looked worried. 'What if Uncle finds out we've spent the money?'

'No worries, nipper. We won't be seeing Uncle Bert for a long time. Come on, we'll go to the pie shop.'

'My foot hurts, Sam. Will you carry me?'

'It's all that dancing,' I said and lifted him onto my shoulders. He was so skinny these days he barely weighed anything.

We left the room and set off down the staircase where women were sitting holding babies and smoking their pipes. It was late when they came out to chat while the kids ran wild, racing up and down, dodging each other and shouting fit to raise the dead.

'Make way!' I called as we tried to reach the bottom.

'Oh look! Here come the gingerbreads,' guffawed one of the women perched on the bottom step. Me and Eliza were used to it but Alfie hated being called that. I'd tried to teach him not to mind; anyway, what's wrong with having red hair? That's what I say.

'Going to the penny gaff?' called another woman.

Her neighbour clapped her hands and yelled, 'Oh lawks! You young gents have forgotten your top hats.' And they all roared. There weren't no harm in it. It were just their bit of fun.

When we stepped outside, it was drizzling. The pie shop was a ten-minute walk away but I knew a short cut off Old Pye Street and down an narrow alley that ran along the back of the One Tun pub.

We passed the brick wall surrounding the yard where Will Beddows held the rat-baiting contests. Rats were delivered regularly by the local rat catcher, Jack Black, and put in cages. Customers came from all over to see a fight and the rats were put into the yard along with a dog or two. I couldn't understand why folk liked it. Watching one animal kill another was sickening.

The fights were still going on that night. Behind the wall, we could hear the men shouting and a jeering. 'Go on, boy. Kill, kill, kill!' Dogs were growling and barking while the rats scrabbled and squealed as they fought.

Alfie clapped his hands over his ears. 'I don't like it, Sam. Go faster!' There were tears in Eliza's eyes too, so I did my best to move quickly and I was glad when we turned into a narrow street where Missus Abdale's pie shop was open from early morning until late at night. I'd been there lots of times and had learned that Missus Abdale had been baking pies since she was a girl. Now she was old with straggly grey hair and cheeks that were red from the heat of the oven, but her pies were the best in town. As we walked into the shop, there was just one customer at the counter. It was a lady of around forty, I think, and no taller than Eliza. She had a brown shawl around her shoulders exactly the same colour as her hair which was swept up on top of her head.

'Two pies, Missus Sackman,' said Missus Abdale, putting them on the counter.

'Thank you,' said the customer who handed over the money and put the pies in her basket. She walked over to the door and, seeing it was still drizzling, she pulled her shawl over her head before stepping outside.

The shawl must have snagged on her necklace and, when she'd gone, Alfie spotted it lying on the floor near to the door of the shop. 'Look!' he said pointing to it. 'That lady dropped something.'

Missus Abdale leaned over the counter and stared at the gold necklace. I lifted Alfie off my shoulder and bent down to pick it up.

'Run after her, Sam,' said Eliza. 'Quick or she'll be gone.'

So Eliza stayed with Alfie while I went to look for the owner of the gold chain. Although the street was dark, the moon came out from behind the clouds and I saw the woman hurrying home, carrying her basket. I ran to catch up with her. But as I got nearer, she started to run too. She must have thought I was a cut-throat or a robber.

She ran faster, glancing over her shoulder, but I called, 'Stop, missus. I've found your necklace.'

As soon as she heard this, she stood still and turned round, panting and looking nervous. 'You dropped it in the pie shop, missus,' I said, running up to her and holding out the gold chain.

She stared at me and touched her neck where the missing chain must've been. Then she looked down at it in my hand as if she couldn't believe it. 'I thought you was a thief, lad. I thought you was going to snatch my basket.'

I shook my head and gave her the necklace.

'Well, there's not many in Devil's Acre would do that. I must say I'm very surprised you brought it back, lad. Thank you.' And she nodded and hurried away.

When I returned to the pie shop, Missus Abdale was smiling. 'You're an honest lad, I'll say that for you. Fancy giving a gold chain back like that.'

'It were only right, Missus Abdale,' I said.

'Fair's fair,' said Alfie which made Missus Abdale smile all the more.

'That's what our ma and pa taught us,' Eliza added.

'Could we have three penny pies, please?' I said. 'I'm starving.'

Eliza took three pennies from the pocket in her apron and placed them on the counter. 'We're all starving hungry,' she said.

Missus Abdale nodded and took the money. 'And you shall have an extra one after your good deed. They're just baked, my loves,' she said, opening the oven door. 'I put a fresh batch in earlier so they'd be ready for the men when they leave the pubs. We usually get busy about then.'

She picked up a cloth and lifted out a huge tray with three rows of golopshus meat pies on it. My mouth was already watering at the thought of tasting 'em.

'Have you brought your basket, my love?' she asked Eliza.

Eliza shook her head. 'I ain't got one, Missus Abdale. We'll carry them home, thank you.'

Missus A frowned. 'Can't have that, deary. You'll get your fingers burned.' And she went and found a piece of cloth and wrapped the pies in it. 'That's better,' she said, handing the parcel to Eliza, 'and by the time you get home they'll be cool enough to eat.'

We thanked Missus Abdale and set off, looking forward to having our warm pies later. There was still drizzle in the air as we turned into the alley that ran past the back of the One Tun. Now there was no shouting or cheering and the barking and squeaking had stopped.

'It's quiet,' I said. 'I reckon the rat baiting's over for the night.'

'Thank goodness,' said Eliza. 'But I expect somebody's lost a lot of money.'

'Like Uncle Bert?' asked Alfie who was riding high on my shoulders again.

As we drew near to the One Tun, the door that led from the yard and into the alley was flung open and a man yelled, 'Get out of here, you useless piece of vermin.'

64

It was Will Beddows, the landlord who was well known around Devil's Acre for his terrible temper – the man Uncle Bert owed money to. We stopped in our tracks as he suddenly hurled a small bundle into the alley and then he went back into the yard, slamming the door behind him.

I wondered if it might be something we could sell and ran to look with Eliza following behind. But what we found was a little black and white dog lying on the ground, his mouth open panting for air.

The nipper slipped off my shoulders and kneeled beside him. 'He's hurt, Sam. Look at him.'

I bent down to get a closer look. 'He's a ratter,' I said. 'He's been bitten real bad. All round the neck and along his back, see.'

'Not much of a ratter, are you, boy?' said Eliza, holding out her hand to stroke him. But the poor thing growled as if he was afraid.

'Leave him,' I said. 'His front leg's hurt real bad. He'll be dead before long. Let's go home.'

But Alfie wasn't having any of it. 'I ain't leavin' him,' he said keeping close to the injured animal as if he was set on staying all night.

'We can't look after a dog, Alfie,' I said. 'I'm tellin' you. Just leave him there. Come on.'

But Alfie grabbed hold of my leg. 'I want to take him home, Sam. Just for tonight. I can look after him. He's hurt.'

Eliza, who was crouching near to Alfie, looked up. 'What's the harm for one night, Sam? He ain't much more than a pup.

Give him a chance, eh? We can do as we please now, can't we? We haven't got Auntie and Uncle telling us what to do.'

It was two against one and, if truth be known, I felt sorry for the little pup. So I agreed we could take the dog home. 'For one night only,' I said. 'After that, he's out on the street and looking after himself, right?'

Eliza grinned. 'Right. Just one night.'

She pulled the parcel of pies from under her arm, unwrapped them and passed them over to me. 'You hold 'em, Sam. They're not so hot now.' Then she used the cloth which was warm from the pies to wrap round the little dog. He growled at first but then let her pick him up and stayed still. As she carried him the rest of the way to the lodging house, he closed his eyes and fell asleep.

Eleven

One dog and three good legs

When we reached home, I was surprised to see Eliza pull a stub of candle and a box of matches from her pocket.

'I nicked 'em from the match factory,' she grinned when she saw me looking puzzled. 'They didn't pay my wages, see.'

I agreed it was only fair. Though it wasn't much pay for two days' work.

While Alfie was settling the dog in the corner, Eliza whispered, 'You don't think them men'll come back tonight, do yer?'

'They might not come at all now they've got our box,' I said. 'It's silver. It must be worth a lot.'

'But what about Grandpa's address?' she said.

That worried me, too. 'We'll talk about it later, eh? When Alfie's asleep.'

She nodded and, with the dog settled, we all sat on the bed and ate the pies at breakneck speed seeing as how we hadn't eaten all day.

'Right,' said Eliza brushing the crumbs from her skirt. 'I'll wash the pup's wounds now. Fetch some water, will yer, Sam?'

Alfie tugged her sleeve. 'It won't hurt him, will it?'

'Course not,' she said. 'It'll help him get better.'

I picked up the tin mugs and went down to the yard where an old wooden barrel was set against a drain pipe collecting water off the roof. It was usually topped with green scum and dead flies floated on it – sometimes you'd find a dead rat in there, as well. If you used it to wash your clothes, they weren't much cleaner when you'd finished.

To get clean water, you had to walk down to the stand pipe in Duck Lane. But by then it was too late to walk that far. The water barrel would have to do. I pushed the scum to one side and dipped the mugs into the water below. I picked out two dead flies but nothing else and went back up our room.

Alfie stroked the pup while Eliza dipped Missus Abdale's cloth into one of the mugs and wiped away the blood from his coat as gentle as she could. The poor thing was curled up like a good un, sleeping soundly so he hardly noticed. The fight at the One Tun must have been real nasty cos there was a good deal of blood to clean off. I expect he was too young to know how to kill rats. He'd lost the fight and nearly lost his life.

Eliza finished the job, blew out the candle and we all climbed onto the bed, too tired by then to talk about anything – let alone how we would survive in Devil's Acre.

We soon fell asleep, but before it was light the next morning, Alfie woke us. 'I want to see the pup,' he said, shaking our shoulders. 'Get up! Get up!'

The two of us moaned a bit but Eliza got out of bed, lit the candle and went over to the corner with Alfie who bent over to see if the dog was still breathing.

'He's alive,' he shouted. 'His eyes are open! Come and look, Sam.' He kneeled by the pup who was lying, staring up at him with big brown eyes.

'He'll need something to drink,' said Eliza and picked one of the tin mugs off the floor and held it to the dog's mouth.

'That's no good,' I said as I slipped out of bed. 'His little tongue ain't long enough. Pour some water into my hands so he can get to it.' I cupped my hands together, Eliza poured a few drops into them and I held them close to the pup's mouth. 'See if you can manage this, boy.'

We all watched as he raised his head and slowly pushed out his tongue until it reached the water and, slowly, he began to lap.

'He's drinking!' said Alfie grinning like he'd found a sixpence. 'He's going to be all right, ain't he, Sam?'

Last night, I thought the pup was sure to die. But now it seemed like he was on the mend. He was a brave little thing. A real fighter. 'Maybe he'll get better,' I said. 'But his front leg's hurt, remember. It might never be straight again. He'll have to learn to walk on three legs.'

'He'll manage,' said Alfie and he went and scrambled under the bed. 'I saved him some pie last night.' And he came out holding a small piece of crust with some meat attached. 'I thought he'd be hungry.'

Eliza shook her head. 'Don't know if he's well enough for meat pie,' she said.

But there was no stopping Alfie. 'I'll tear it into bits for him,' he said and settled next to the animal, breaking off a crumb of pastry and carefully placing it in his mouth. Then he stroked his head gently and said, 'Come on, boy. You eat that. You'll like, you will.' The dog gazed up at him before closing his mouth and swallowing the crumb – our Alfie had always had a way with animals.

'He's eatin' it! See. He likes it!' And he broke off another piece of pastry, which the dog took straight away as if he knew now that Alfie was his friend and wouldn't hurt him.

'He's trying to sit up,' said Eliza. 'He wants more. Look at his little tail. It's starting to wag.'

It was true. The pup was licking his lips and looking better already and in time, by feeding him bits of pie and drinks of water, he sat up and allowed Alfie to pet him.

'He'll have to go out,' I said.

'No!' Alfie shouted. 'He's not leavin' here till he's well.'

'Calm down, nipper,' I said. 'I just meant that he'll need to pee after drinking that water, won't he? I'll go with yer. The slop bucket needs emptying anyway.'

Alfie cradled the dog in his arms and walked slowly and carefully down the stairs. I followed behind carrying the slop bucket, which hadn't been emptied for days and stank something shocking.

It was barely light by then. There was nobody in the yard except a costermonger seeing to his cart.

'Mornin', lad,' he said to Alfie. 'What you got there?'

'A dog. We're looking after it.'

'Oh, are you?' he laughed. 'Well, a ratter like him won't be no trouble. He'll feed himself, won't he? I expect he'll bring home a handsome rat for your tea. Very tasty, rat stew!' And he threw his head back and roared with laughter. Then he set off for market, pushing his empty barrow which he'd fill up with fish and then sell in a more respectable area.

I left Alfie with the pup and took the slop bucket over to the rubbish heap near the water butt and flung the contents over it.

'How's he doing, Alfie?' I called across the yard, 'Has he peed yet?'

He nodded. The pup was standing on his three good legs shivering with cold until Alfie picked him up ever so gently and carried him inside.

'What are we going to do now, Sam?' Eliza asked while Alfie sat and stroked the pup. 'We ain't got Ma's box no more. So how will we find Grandpa now? We ain't got that letter with his address?'

'I should have read it and remembered it,' I said, feeling angry with myself. I looked away, shrugging my shoulders. 'Maybe we don't need to find him. I can look after you, can't I? I'm fourteen. I'm old enough to do men's work. I'll find a building site or another railway track or something. We don't need nobody.'

'That's stupid, Sam,' she whispered, not wanting Alfie to hear us quarrelling. 'Grandpa can look after us. He's rich. We'll have a grand life away from here. We'll have blankets on the bed and as much food as we want and warm clothes and—'

'Forget him. What's the good of looking for him when we don't even know where he lives.' I waited a minute, thinking.

'Anyway, he never wanted to see us, did he? Not when we was little. Not now. Not never. Why would he want us living with him? Answer me that, Eliza Pargeter.'

'But—'

'We can manage by ourselves. I'll look after us, so don't say no more about it.'

Eliza slapped her hands on her hips and glared at me. 'You'll look after us, will you? And how are you going to do that?'

Twelve

Men's work

We had a right old shindy, Eliza and me. *She* thought I couldn't look after us. *I* thought I could.

'I won't have to give my earnings to Uncle Bert to spend on beer and gambling,' I told her. 'I'll find some proper work.'

Alfie, whose ears must have been flapping, suddenly sat up. 'You goin' to find work, Sam? I'll come with you. I can work, can't I?'

'No, Alfie,' I said. 'You're only six. I'm going to get real men's work.'

I didn't wait for any more arguments; I wrapped my muffler tight round my neck and said, 'You look after Alfie, Eliza. I'll be back with some money and there'll be food in our bellies tonight, I promise.' And with that I walked out of the door.

I left Devil's Acre and set off up Victoria Street heading towards Hyde Park. I'd heard that a grand new building for something called the Great Exhibition was being built there. It was supposed to open next year but everybody said it couldn't be done. I hadn't seen it myself but they said it was made of glass, which seemed a bit daft to me. I was sure there was work to be had there. Some men in the rookeries were talking about it.

So I hurried towards the park. I had responsibilities, I did. And I was going to get a man's job.

Away from Devil's Acre, the roads were wider and cleaner, there were no cess pits and no crumbling houses, only fine buildings and people riding in carriages and omnibuses. There was plenty of noise from the traffic and the street sellers, shouting their wares. But there were trees along the way and I breathed the fresh air that reminded me of home with Ma and Pa.

It was a long walk to the end of Victoria Street and when I carried on up Grosvenor Place I passed the gardens at the back of Buckingham Palace. I felt cheery knowing that Queen Victoria might be near – probably having her breakfast. So I waved, just in case she was looking out of the window.

Once I arrived at Hyde Park Corner, I could see the park across the way. There was the frame of the new building. Crikes! It was massive. Iron columns. Dozens of 'em. I stood and stared. I'd never seen anything like it. They must need hundreds of workers to build it, I thought. But as I hurried on I saw a long line of men snaking into the distance. There must have been a hundred or more ahead of me. It was a shock, I can tell you. If they were all wanting to be taken on, I didn't stand much of a chance. But what else could I do? I joined the line.

The men looked much the same in corduroy trousers and waistcoats, with neckerchiefs round their necks and cloth caps on their heads – just like the men from the railway track. I could tell by the way they talked that many were Irish, and it didn't surprise me. I knew it was easier to find work here than in Ireland. I'd heard from Paddy and the Irish workers in Camden that their home country was in a sorry state after the potato famine.

'Are you hoping to get work, young un?' asked the man in front of me.

I pulled myself to my full height. 'I am.'

The man was as tall as a house and he looked down at me and grinned.

'Have you worked on a building site before, son?' he asked.

'No. But I worked on the railway.'

Then he smiled in a kindly way but he shook his head. 'You don't look too strong, lad. You can't be more than twelve, I'm guessing.'

What a cheek! I knew I was skinny – but did he really think I was only twelve?

'I'm nearly fifteen.' I puffed out my chest, hoping to make myself look bigger and older.

'Well, you don't look it and if the gaffers think you're twelve, they'll not take you on. Too young to work more than six hours, see. That's the law.'

The men standing further down the queue must have heard him. 'That's right,' one of them said. Then he glanced down at my skinny arms and legs. 'Have you left your muscles at home?' And they all laughed.

'You need muscles of steel to work here, lad,' said another

one 'You're as thin as a stick. You'll not last an hour on a building site.'

The man nearest to me must have understood how miserable I was feeling. 'I tell you, sonny,' he said quietly, 'we've been here an hour already but we'll be lucky if we get work today. Believe me, I've been here every day now for weeks. You'd best go home to your mammy or find yourself a nice chimney to sweep.'

I took a deep breath and looked up at the man. 'Right,' I said, as bold as you like. 'I ain't goin' to waste my time standing here, mister. If I can't get no work, I'll look somewhere else. I'm off.' And I stepped out of the queue and marched away, not knowing where to go.

All that day, I tried to get work. How could I go back without money? I'd promised Eliza we'd have food tonight. I walked all the way to the market at Covent Garden and did some sweeping up of vegetables scraps that the porters had dropped early that day and they paid me two pennies and gave me a baked potato. I tried to find more work but there was nothing doing. Too many people. Not enough jobs.

Thirteen

A visit from Mister Devitt

By the time I arrived home I was worn out from walking here, there and everywhere trying to find work.

Alfie came running to the door, yelling, 'Sam! Sam! Look at the dog. Look! He can run on three legs! Look at him.'

The black and white dog was standing by me, wagging his tale and wanting my attention. But I was feeling real dumpish. 'Take him away, Alfie,' I said, flopping onto the bed. 'I ain't in no mood for playing.'

'But he's better now, Sam. We went and got a penny worth of bread this morning and Eliza begged a spoonful of milk from Missus O'Donnell what lives downstairs. And we broke up the bread and dropped it in the milk and...'

I sat up. 'You spent a penny on that dog?' I shouted. 'A penny? I've been out all day and I've only earned two.' I pulled the pennies out of my pocket and flung them onto the bed. 'Why did I bother, eh?'

Alfie, seeing I was in a grump, picked up the pup and went to sit with him in the corner.

'It's no use shouting, Sam,' Eliza said. 'The dog didn't have all the bread, you know. There's enough left for the three of

77

us and I got some herrings too. I paid with that money we made singing.'

I didn't reply. I was just too tired.

'I've been up to Duck Lane and fetched some fresh water this morning,' she said picking a tin mug off the table and handed it to me. 'Here, drink this and you'll feel better.'

I leaned on my elbows and raised myself up, and took a mouthful.

'That dog's got to go,' I said, looking straight at Alfie. 'I told you last night, we can't keep him. Now go and put him out.'

'No!' Alfie shouted, his eyes brimming with tears. 'I ain't putting him out. He's mine and I gave him a name and everything. He's called Patch.'

I swung my legs off the bed, ready to grab the dog. I might not have found work, I thought, but I could show 'em who was boss in this family.

Eliza was having none of it. 'Stop it, Sam. There ain't no need for you to go bullying our Alfie. Let's have some herrings, eh? Then we'll talk about what to do.'

Before I could answer, there was a loud knocking at the door. A particular kind of knocking. I looked at Eliza and she looked at me. There was only one person who knocked like that. The rent collector, Mister Devitt.

'We'll ignore it, eh?' said Eliza in a whisper.

When we didn't open the door, he knocked again, louder this time, and he called out, 'I know somebody's in there and if you don't open this door, I'll kick it down.'

Alfie kept hold of Patch and cowered on the corner. I went to the door and opened it.

'Oh good evening, Mister Devitt,' I said in my most polite voice. 'Come in, if you will.'

Mister Devitt marched in, looking round the room. He was a small weasel of a man with thin lips and a long, narrow nose. 'Well, where is he?' he demanded.

'Who are you looking for, Mister Devitt?' asked Eliza, looking as innocent as a newborn babe.

The rent collector glowered at her. 'I'm looking for Bert Bagstone, of course. He owes me nine shillings for three weeks' rent. Now, where is he? I've had enough of his lies.'

'He ain't here, Mister Devitt,' I insisted. 'He's gone with our auntie to see his father who lives in...er...the country. He's very old, see, and ever so sick. In fact, he's like to die.'

'Yes,' said Eliza. 'They left yesterday and we're at our wits' end. We're on our own with not a penny to our name and we don't know when they'll be back. What can we do, Mister Devitt?'

The rent collector narrowed his eyes, suspicious like. 'I don't believe a word,' he said. 'I want my money! No excuses.'

'But we ain't got no money,' I told him.

Then he raised his chin and sniffed the air. 'If you've got no money, why can I smell fresh herring? How did you buy 'em, eh?'

'They were only a penny from the costermonger,' said Eliza.

'Only a penny? But that penny belongs to me by rights!'

he shouted, thumping his fist on the table so that it wobbled and nearly collapsed.

Eliza stood in front of him, her arms folded across her chest. 'And your sort would have us starve, wouldn't you? You'd take the herrings out of our mouths, you would.'

The rent collector was furious. 'You spent my money, missy. Don't you speak to me like that.' Then he grabbed Eliza's arm. I dashed forward to stop him but he struck me with his other hand and I staggered backwards and fell to the floor.

Alfie started screaming. Patch started yapping. Mister Devitt yelled, 'Out onto the street all of you. Out where you belong! NOW!'

I lay there with my head spinning certain that we were finished. But I'd reckoned without the three-legged pup. He went straight for the rent collector and sank his teeth into his leg.

'Get him off! Get him off!' yelled Mister Devitt, hopping around on one leg while Patch hung onto the other and would not let go. He screamed blue murder. He yelled for help. The whole lodging house must have heard but nobody came. Nobody liked the rent collector, see.

When Alfie finally called the dog off, Mister Devitt staggered out onto the landing, blood oozing through his trouser leg vowing that he would be back within the hour with a gang of strong-armed men.

Fourteen

The One Tun

Eliza sat on the floor with her arm round Alfie who was stroking Patch and telling him what a clever dog he was.

'Devitt will be back with his men to throw us out,' I said, looking glumly out of the window. 'I didn't find work, Eliza, and we've no money. What are we going to do? Do we go to the workhouse now?'

'You tried to look after us, Sam, you done your best,' Eliza said. 'I know you don't think Grandpa will want us, but he might. He's the only family we got. We should try to find him.'

I turned to look at her. '*How* do we find him? We don't know where he lives. The address was in Ma's box, remember. Our grandpa might live miles from here. He might live in another country.'

'We could find out.'

'How?'

Eliza sat on the edge of the bed. 'Remember them two rogues what took Ma's box?'

'Course, I do.'

'They were takin' it to the One Tun, weren't they? Going to

give it to the landlord?'

I was hardly listening. I was thinking if I couldn't get us out of this mess then she couldn't. Nobody could.

'We could go and find the box, Sam. Get that letter with our grandpa's address on it.'

I stared at her. 'Go to the One Tun? Are you mad or something? Them rogues drink at that pub. They're two of Beddows's thugs. If they see us, Eliza, they'll beat us up.'

She grinned at me. 'They won't be there, knuckle head. They said they were going up Battersea pigeon shooting today. They won't be back yet.'

'Well I ain't going to the One Tun. It's full of thieves and murderers. We could get our throats slit!'

'That's just gossip and I ain't scared,' she said.

I thought about it for a minute. She had a point.

'There's sure to be a room where Will Beddows lives with his missus,' I said. 'He'll have put the box in a cupboard or something.'

'You could just take the letters out, Sam. He'll never miss 'em,' said Eliza.

I was beginning to see the possibilities. Though I say it myself, it wasn't a bad plan – for a girl.

'If you start singing, Eliza, you can make a real shindig.'

'Can I dance again?' Alfie piped up.

But I didn't want him in there. 'No. It's too dangerous, nipper. You'll have to wait outside.'

Eliza nodded. 'I'll go in on my own, but I can still make a lot of noise...'

'... and I'll do the dangerous stuff of looking for the box,' I said.

'Scared, are yer?'

'Who's scared? Beddows will only beat me to a frazzle if he catches me. Will you come to my funeral, eh?'

Eliza laughed. 'You won't get caught, Sam. When l start singing everybody will be looking at me and that's when you slip into the back room, see.'

I thought there was just a chance that it would work. 'All right,' I said. 'We'll do it. Come on. Let's get out of here before Devitt comes back with his heavy mob.'

We started collecting the few things we had. Eliza picked up an old bonnet that belonged to Aunt Maud and the shawl she had dropped in her hurry to get away. I put Pa's copy of *Oliver Twist* in my pocket. If I had that, I'd always have something to read no matter how poor we were.

'I want Uncle Bert's top hat,' said Alfie. 'He dropped it when he climbed through the window. He won't want it any more, will he?'

'You have it, nipper,' I said, and popped it on his head.

It was much too big for him and slipped down over his eyes but he liked it. 'Now I'm a gent,' he said and we had to laugh.

There was nothing else to take with us and when we were ready to go I took a deep breath and said, 'We can't take the dog with us, Alfie. We've got enough problems looking after ourselves.'

Eliza gave me a black look and Alfie glared at me.

'I'll look after him,' he said. 'I got a piece of rope from Missus O'Donnell this mornin'.' He tied a loop and slipped it round the dog's neck.

I should have put my foot down. I should have made him leave the dog behind, but I couldn't. The pup was brave. He'd scared off the rent collector for us, after all. I suppose he deserved to stay with us.

'Just make sure you keep your eye on him,' I told Alfie. 'Let's hope he'll find himself a nice juicy rat.'

Eliza put on Aunt Maud's bonnet and pulled the shawl over her old worn one. Now the room was empty except for the wooden bed, the rickety table and the cold air that whipped through the broken window.

Once we were out in alley, we felt the bitter wind of winter on our faces as we walked to the top of Old Pye Street and turned in the direction of the One Tun.

'You stay away from the pub, Alfie,' I said. 'Somebody might see Patch and they'll know he's one of Beddows's ratters.'

He promised faithfully that he would wait down the street. 'Don't move,' I said. 'We'll be back in no time.'

Fifteen

The silver box

Eliza tucked her hair under the bonnet and pulled the woollen shawl around her shoulders. 'Do I look fine, Sam?' she said, grinning at me. 'Wait five minutes before you come in.'

She pushed the door open and disappeared into the pub while I was left outside in the cold, my heart thumping, hoping she'd be all right.

But Eliza was a real plucky girl and it wasn't long before I heard her singing 'Silvia's Song' as sweet as you like. She must have persuaded Beddows to let her do a turn and I wondered what tale she told him. She could spin a yarn could our Eliza.

Halfway through her song, I took a deep breath to calm the collywobbles and slipped inside the One Tun. The pub was a noisy, smoky place packed mostly with men puffing pipes and drinking beer after a day's work at the market or on a building site. In the corner there were four women. One of 'em was dolled up to the nines. The others were old and dressed in faded black, chattering like jackdaws over a glass of gin.

I pressed my back to the wall, hoping nobody would notice me. Eliza was over the far side standing on a chair and singing away with a smile on her face. Good old Eliza!

While she sang, I glanced around the room looking for a door that might lead to Beddows's living quarters. It wasn't difficult to spot cos there was only one. The trouble was that the door was behind the bar. Oh lawks! How could I go through it when the landlord was leaning on the bar with his wife standing next to him?

I caught Eliza's eye and she must have understood the problem because when she'd finished her song and the men finally stopped cheering and throwing pennies into her bonnet, she started another. This time it was lively with a rollicking chorus. The customers loved it. They joined in with gusto, waving their glasses of ale and thumping their fists on the table in time to the music until Will Beddows stepped out from behind the bar to make sure nothing got out of hand.

The song grew noisier, the chorus louder and Eliza looked over at the landlord's wife behind the bar and beckoned her.

'Won't you join us, Missus Beddows?' she called. 'I expect you can dance like the best of 'em. Come and show us how.' Then she said, as bold as you please, 'You'd like that, lads, wouldn't yer?'

The men roared and shouted, 'Come and show us, missus. Give us a turn!' And even Missus Beddows, who was built like a wrestler, seemed pleased to be asked. She stepped out from behind the bar, raised her skirt above her ankles and began a jig, bouncing around like an enormous rubber ball while Eliza sang and the customers clapped and shouted.

Thanks, Eliza! I thought. Now that Beddows and his wife were away from the bar, I could make a move. Sweat broke out on my forehead at the thought of anyone seeing me. My heart was pounding faster than ever and the collywobbles were back. But I had to go and look for the box. I couldn't stand in a corner all night, doing nothing.

While Missus Beddows twirled and jigged and the customers stamped their boots in time to the singing, I squeezed past 'em, hoping nobody would notice me creep behind the bar. I lifted the latch of the door and slipped through sharpish, shutting it behind me. But instead of the landlord's back parlour, I found myself standing in a narrow corridor with three doors. Two on the left and one on the right. *Which way now?* I thought. I didn't have much time. I had to get back into the pub before the song finished and Beddows returned to the bar or I'd be trapped. Which door should I open? One, two or three? Holding my breath, I went for number three, the one on the right. I pushed it open and saw that I was in the parlour. Jammy, eh?

Quickly I glanced around looking for the most likely place where the box might be. Everything was as neat as a new pin – armchairs, a table with a red cloth. Beddows clearly wasn't short of money. I could see that. He'd probably made it from the rat baiting in the yard. I soon spotted what I was looking for. Set against the far wall was a fine mahogany sideboard with two cupboards. If the box was anywhere, it would be there, I was sure.

I opened the first cupboard and found a teapot and six cups and saucers covered in rosebuds. Ma would have loved 'em. But there was no silver box. Just as I was searching through the second cupboard, Eliza's song came to an end and the customers cheered and clapped. My time was up. I had to leave before Beddows went back to the bar. I stood up and ran for the door.

And I came face to face with the landlord's wife.

Sixteen

Caught!

Missus Beddows was terrifying up close. She had muscles like turnips which she must have developed from rolling barrels of beer.

I tried to push past her but – no chance! She grabbed hold of my jacket collar.

'What you doin' here, lad?' she said, lifting me off the ground and shaking me like a terrier with a rabbit. 'A thief, are yer? Trying to steal our hard-earned money, eh?'

I didn't answer because I couldn't. She was holding me that tight I could hardly breathe. Then she shouted for her husband. 'Beddows! Come here quick!'

I was making terrible choking noises when the landlord burst in. He was even more scary than his wife – what with his chin covered in whiskers and eyebrows so thick and black you could hardly see his eyes. 'What's up, Missus?' he snapped.

Missus Beddows let go of my collar and I collapsed in a heap on the floor. 'He's been looking in our sideboard. Little thief!'

I couldn't deny it. I'd left the door open.

Will Beddows's face turned black as thunder. He was well known around Devil's Acre for his temper and I'd already met the men he'd sent after Uncle Bert, so I was shaking something terrible, thinking that he was going to chop me up and feed me to the rats. My stomach was churning and I would have been sick if there'd been anything in it to throw up.

Beddows bent down, grabbed hold of my nose and pulled me to my feet. 'Who are you?' he growled. 'What you up to in my parlour?'

I opened my mouth to answer but no sound came out.

'Speak up, lad, or you'll feel my belt across your back.'

In the end, I managed to say, 'I . . . I'm Sam,' which isn't easy when your nose is squeezed between somebody's fingers.

'Well, Sam whatever-your-name-is, you look like a thief to me. What were you after, eh? Money, was it?'

'A . . . a box, sir.'

The landlord let go of my nose. 'A box? What kind of box?'

'A silver box some men took from us yesterday.'

A nasty smile crept across his face. 'Now I get it. You're Bert Bagstone's lad, ain't yer? A real chip off the old block!'

'He's not my pa,' I protested. 'He's my uncle. We've lived with him since our ma died.'

Beddows snorted. 'Well, your uncle's a rogue who's too fond of his beer and his gambling.' Then he gripped my shoulder which hurt something shocking. 'He owes me money, lad. Did he send you to get the box?'

I shook my head. Seeing I had no other choice, I thought I'd better tell the truth. 'Uncle Bert's run off. I don't really want the box. I just want the letters inside it, see. Could you let me have 'em, please, sir? You can keep the box.'

'Oh can I?' he said, squeezing my shoulder so hard that I yelled out loud, which didn't seem to bother him one bit. 'I can keep it, can I? Well, that's real generous,' he sneered. 'But you're too late, boy. I don't have no box. I took it to the pawn shop this morning and got five shillings for it.'

My heart sank and my shoulders drooped. The silver box was gone. He'd sold it.

'Feeling bad, are yer?' said Will Beddows. 'Well, you'll be feeling worse before long. I don't like folks breaking into my property, see.' He raised his fist ready to throw a punch and I shut my eyes, praying that the pain wouldn't be too bad.

Then someone burst into the room.

'Come quick, Mister Beddows. There's a fight going on and they'll break up the pub unless you come and put a stop to it. They're smashing the place up.'

It was Eliza.

Beddows flung me away and dashed out of the room while Eliza burst into tears and grabbed hold of his wife's arm.

'Oh, I'm that scared, Missus Beddows. Truly I am,' she sobbed. 'I was only singing to get a few pennies to take to my poor, sick ma.' She sniffed and wiped her nose on her sleeve. 'Them men's dangerous. I want to go home.'

'No need to get yourself into a stew, girl. You stick by me. I'll see you get out of here. You won't come to no harm.'

Eliza gave her a tearful smile. 'Thank you, Missus Beddows. That's kind, that is.'

91

The landlord's wife put her arms around Eliza, walked out of the room and shut the door. But in two seconds, she flung it open again and wagged her finger at me. 'Don't you move, my lad. My husband will be back to sort you out.' She pulled a key from her pocket, slammed the door shut and locked it.

Now what? Beddows would be back any minute. Lawks a mercy! He'd beat me to a pulp for sure. I looked around the room for a way of escape and saw a small window next to the fireplace, overlooking the yard at the back of the pub. I thought it was big enough for me to climb through but when I tried to open it, it wouldn't budge. I tried again but it was stuck fast. There was nothing for it – I'd have to break the glass. I felt bad about causing damage. Ma wouldn't like it. 'Sorry, Ma,' I said out loud and picked up the poker from the hearth, swinging it at the window and smashing it into a hundred pieces. It made a terrible noise. Somebody must have heard. 'Hurry, Sam, hurry!' I said to myself. 'Get out fast before they come.'

I grabbed the cloth off the table, wrapped it round my hand and pushed the biggest pieces of glass away. Even then, climbing through was a nightmare. My trousers got caught and were torn bad in several places. Lawks! Eliza would give me a right earwigging. She got fed up with sewing and patching.

I dropped down into the yard. It was dark, but I could hear a rustling and a squeaking and a squawking. Straight away I knew what it was. Rats! Over by the wall there were two crates of 'em waiting for the next rat-baiting contest. I wasn't scared or nothing. They were in their cages and I felt sorry for them, see. They'd probably be dead by tomorrow.

But I had a brilliant idea. Behind me was a door that led back into the pub. I went over and pushed it open and then quickly undid the catches on the cages. The rats swarmed out – black ones, grey ones, fat ones, thin ones – dozens and dozens of 'em, glad to be free. Some ran over my feet, some scurried round and round the yard until they found the open door. Then they did what I wanted 'em to do. They escaped into the One Tun.

I wish I could have seen Beddows's face when the rats invaded his pub. I wish I could have heard his customers screaming and cursing and yelling. Jumping up onto the seats, climbing onto the tables, afraid of being bitten. But I didn't wait to see it all. I ran out of the gate that led into the back alleyway and I disappeared into the night.

Seventeen

Going to the Lyceum

'Where you been?' Alfie demanded when I finally met up with him. 'I'm freezing. Me and Eliza's been waiting ages.'

Eliza laughed and pulled a face at me. 'Sorry you got locked in like that.'

'Well, I'm here now, ain't I?' I said. 'Let's get away from here, sharpish. Somebody might come after us.'

I picked Alfie up and raced down Olde Pye Street and into Strutton Ground, only stopping when we were a long way from the One Tun.

'Rest a bit,' I gasped and we leaned against a wall, glad for the chance to get our breath back. While we stood there, I told them about letting the rats into the One Tun. They bent double laughing.

'Now they know how them rats feel,' said Alfie. 'Wish I could have seen 'em.'

But I was wanting to hear Eliza's story.

'How did you persuade Beddows to let you sing, Eliza? He's a real hard nut, he is.'

Eliza grinned. 'I told him I was a poor girl trying to make a living by singing, but he wasn't interested, the old misery.

Told me to leave, he did.'

'So what did you do?'

'I started to blub, see. Not too much. Just a few tears running down my cheeks. I told him my poor old mother was sick and like to die and how I needed to earn some money to take care of her. After that, he said, I could stay "Just this once". If you ask me, Will Beddows ain't as hard as he makes out.'

'No,' I said. 'He's a thug and I've got the bruises to prove it. Lucky you came when you did. I thought Beddows was going to kill me.'

She winked at me. 'I saw Missus Beddows go out of the door behind the bar, see. Then I heard her yell for her husband and he went running over there. So I knew you were in trouble.'

'Lucky that fight started in the pub.'

'Lucky be blowed!' she said. '*I* made it happen. Knocked over a glass of beer and put the blame on one of the men. One thing led to another and they were soon flinging their fists at each other. It don't take much. They likes fighting, see.'

I laughed. 'Well, you saved me, girl. Thanks.'

Alfie who was sitting on a step stroking Patch, suddenly looked up. 'Did you get the letters, Sam? Can we go to see Grandpa now?'

I shook my head.

'What?' said Eliza, her mouth falling open. 'You mean you didn't find the box? After all that trouble?'

'It weren't my fault,' I said. 'It wasn't there. Beddows said he took it to the pawn shop and got five shillings for it.'

Eliza's face fell. She looked as miserable as a dog with fleas and I thought Alfie was going to burst into tears.

'Cheer up,' I said. 'No point in fretting. We'll work out something.'

Alfie tugged at my sleeve.

'Can't we go to the shop and buy the box?'

Eliza smiled. 'Course we can. I know where the pawn shop is.'

'Can't be done,' I said as I leaned against the wall. 'Where can we get five shillings? We'll never earn that much?'

Eliza punched me on the arm. 'I know.'

'Where?'

'Down the Strand. Them toffs who go to the theatre – they've got money to spare. I've seen 'em. When they come out after the show, I'll sing and Alfie can dance.'

'Patch can dance too!' said Alfie, bouncing up and down with excitement. 'I showed him how to walk on his hind legs. He's good, he is.'

'Then he can join us, Alfie. And Sam can go round with his cap. We'll soon have five shillings, you see if we don't.'

'I don't know nothing about theatres,' I said. 'Where do we find one?'

'I know,' she replied. 'Come on. Let's get movin'. They'll be comin' out after the show before long.'

'How's your foot, nipper?' I asked.

'A bit sore,' he said. 'But I want to dance with Patch. Can I, Sam?'

Eliza made Alfie sit down and she took off the cloth she

had wrapped round his foot yesterday. It was black with dirt already.

'That cut don't look right,' she said. 'It's all swollen. But I'll bind it with some cloth – you'll be nice and comfy, eh?'

She lifted her skirt, tore another piece off her petticoat and wrapped it round his foot making a thick padding. 'Do you think you can dance on that, Alfie?'

He stood up and tested his foot. 'That's better,' he said and smiled. 'I'll help you earn that five shillings.'

We all hurried up Whitehall and along the Strand with Patch walking behind on his lead. The theatre we were heading for was called the Lyceum. Eliza had been there with Aunt Maud last summer to sell flowers to the toffs. They'd bought violets from the market and tied them up in penny bundles. But the weather was too hot and the violets wilted. Shame. Aunt Maud was real upset. They hadn't earned nothing for their trouble.

'Aunt knew all about the Lyceum,' said Eliza, 'She told me it had gas lighting and everything. Imagine!'

'What's gas?' asked Alfie.

'Like them lamps,' she replied, pointing to the lights along the Strand.

'I like candles best,' said Alfie. 'Gas lamps is dangerous.'

'Naw,' laughed Eliza. 'I told you. The Lyceum's a real up-to-date place.'

We turned off the Strand up Wellington Street and walked towards the theatre. It was real grand with columns at the front and steps going up to a huge door. Like a palace, it was.

Two flower sellers were already by the door, waiting to sell lucky heather to the audience when they came out.

'Who's that lot?' asked Alfie, pointing to a group of musicians in front of the theatre.

'Lawks!' said Eliza. 'Whoever they are, that's just where we need to be.'

Eighteen

Joe Bolly

'It's no good, Eliza,' I said. 'We can't stay. That band'll drown out your singing. We'll have to find another theatre.'

'I only know this one.'

I was thinking of finding somebody and asking for help when a boy came striding round the corner, cheerful as you like. He was about my age and wearing a jacket and trousers which were a good deal too big for him with a battered top hat on his head. His boots would have fitted somebody twice his size and were tied with string round his ankles. Even though his clothes weren't the best you've ever seen, he swaggered towards us as if he was a real toff.

'Evening, lady and gents!' he said sweeping off his hat and bowing like we were royalty. 'Joe Bolly's the name. You're strangers round here, ain't yer?'

We nodded.

'Down on yer luck, is yer?' he said.

We nodded again.

'What you doing at the Lyceum, then? Up for a bit of thievin'?'

'No, we're not!' Eliza replied all huffy. 'I was going to sing

99

when they come out of the theatre.'

'And me and my dog were going to do a dance,' said Alfie. 'My dog's called Patch and he's clever, even though he's only got three good legs.'

'He looks very clever to me,' said Joe, grinning. 'But you've got a bit of a problem, ain't yer? Seeing as how that German band's waiting to play. I don't suppose anybody will listen to you. I've heard 'em before and they're very loud – make a fine old din, they do.'

Eliza sighed and shook her head. 'Know anywhere else we can go?'

'Course I do,' he replied. 'But you don't have to go nowhere.' He pointed towards the band who had left their instruments on the ground. They were some way off, leaning against a wall, chatting like fishwives and smoking their pipes.

'See that drum?' said Joe looking at me. 'Go and pick it up.' Then he turned to Eliza and Alfie. 'And you two go and get a trumpet.'

'We can't do that! They're not ours,' I said.

Joe winked in a cocksure kind of a way. 'You're not going to thieve 'em. You just have to make a noise, see.'

'That's daft,' said Eliza. 'What would we do that for?'

He winked again. 'Wait and see, my friends. Just bang and blow as loud as you can. Follow me. I'll show yer.'

Joe swaggered across to the instruments, bold as you like, and grabbed hold of a huge brass thing that was almost as big as he was.

'Oi!' called one of the musicians and waved his hand.

But Joe ignored him and began to blow, making a sound like a pig in pain.

'Join in you lot!' he said as he took a breath. So I grabbed hold of the drum and started banging it and Eliza and Alfie joined in blowing the trumpets as hard as they could. We made a shocking din. It was enough to turn you deaf.

The musicians soon came running towards us. Joe stopped blowing and handed over his instruments as nice as you please and we did the same – though I didn't understand what Joe's plan was. We got a terrible telling-off from the musicians – which didn't matter cos it was all in German and we couldn't understand a word.

'Now scarper!' yelled Joe and we ran away from the theatre and into the next street where we collapsed laughing.

'That was a lark!' said Alfie.

Joe was already on his knees, peeping round the corner. 'Watch,' he said.

We all crouched down and saw the musicians examining their instruments for damage. Then, the front door of the theatre was flung open and the manager in a smart evening suit came rushing down the steps waving frantically at the band. 'How dare you make such a noise,' he shouted. 'We can hear it inside the theatre. You're disturbing the performance.'

The musicians looked at him in amazement. Their leader, who could speak a little English, stepped forward and bowed stiffly to the manager. 'Pardon me, sir. We did not play—'

'No?' said the manager, bristling with anger. 'Pardon *you*, sir. I heard you play. There is no denying it. Now go away! Remove yourselves.'

The leader pointed down the street and tried to explain how some children had made the noise and had run off. But the manager would not listen.

'It was a terrible noise,' he said, flapping his hands. 'I won't have it near my theatre. Now go away at once. Go!'

Without another word, the men picked up their instruments and sloped off, looking miserable. I must admit I felt bad as I watched them disappear into the Strand. They were only trying to make a living, like us.

But Joe was as chirpy as ever. 'Well ain't that a piece o' luck?' he said. 'Now you can have your plum spot where the ladies and gents will see yer when they come out.'

'You're real cunning, you are,' said Eliza. 'Are you coming with us?'

'Naw,' he said. 'I've got business of my own.'

'What's that?'

But Joe just winked and walked away.

Nineteen

The man with the
silk handkerchief

It was some time before the play finished, and while we waited for the toffs to come out, two black horses came galloping down the street pulling a four-wheeled carriage and stopped right there in front of the theatre.

'Lawks!' I said. 'I ain't never seen anything like it.'

It was painted deep blue with gold bits here and there. It was a fine sight, I can tell yer.

'Is it Queen Victoria's?' asked Alfie, hopping about like a jack-in-a-box.

I didn't think so but I was keen to see who was inside.

We stared as a footman in a blue and gold uniform jumped from his place at the back and came to hold the horses steady while the old coachman wearing a heavy greatcoat and a top hat, climbed down from the driving seat to stretch his legs.

But that was only the first carriage to arrive. Before long, the street was full of 'em. There were horses neighing and hooves clattering on cobblestones making a real din. Soon the street was blocked and nobody could move. It was as if the whole of London had sent their carriages to wait in front of the Lyceum.

When the play was finished, the doors of the theatre opened and the audience poured down the steps looking for their carriages to take them home. The gents were real toffs in black evening suits, with bow ties and top hats. As for the ladies... well! They had silk dresses such as you've never seen with embroidered capes over their shoulders.

'Cor!' said Eliza. 'Ain't them frocks bootiful? But how do they get through a door in them wide skirts?'

'How do I know?' I said to Eliza. 'But don't just stand there. Start singing before they get into their carriages!'

She began with a sea shanty 'Spanish Ladies' and Alfie danced in a lively fashion with his arms crossed over his chest and Uncle Bert's top hat wobbling on his head. When he whistled Patch to join in, the little dog jumped around on his hind legs like a real trooper.

It was Patch who stole the show. A girl of twelve or so spotted him and she rushed down the steps ahead of the crowd. 'Do hurry up, Mama,' she called over her shoulder. 'Come and look at the dog. It's dancing!'

'I'm coming, Philomena,' called her mother, lifting the skirt of her long blue dress as she followed her. 'What a clever little dog,' she said and smiled very pleasant like as she watched.

A crowd soon gathered round us, clapping when Eliza finished her song. I was about to offer my cap around in the hope of collecting some money when a large lady, clinging onto the arm of an elderly man came struggling down the steps of the theatre. By the time she had reached the bottom, she was quite out of breath, but somehow she managed to call out, 'Philomena! Emily! No, no, no. Come away!'

The crowd turned to see who was hollering like a common street seller. But the lady didn't seem to care. She pushed her way past several people before grabbing hold of the girl's hand in a very rough manner. 'Come away, Philomena! Do!' she insisted.

'But, Grandmama,' the girl protested. 'I was watching...'

'We leave at once!' the old lady insisted. 'Those children carry dreadful diseases. Look at them. They are so dirty. They are a disgrace. Come!'

Well, the old lady clearly never learned any manners, that's what I say. She dragged her granddaughter through the crowd, followed by the rest of her family. They climbed into the blue and gold carriage which was waiting for them and were driven off down the street.

'Good riddance,' you might say. But that was bad luck for us. Once the girl and her family ran off, there were 'oohs' and 'ahhs' and 'oh dears' as the rest of the crowd stepped away, thinking if they stood too close, they might catch a terrible disease or fleas at the very least.

'Sing!' I called to Eliza. 'Quick before they all go.'

She began again and sang 'Softly, O Midnight Hours' as sweet as any bird. The crowd stayed as Alfie danced, but I noticed his face was screwed up like he was in pain or something. The rag Eliza had wrapped round his foot had come undone and fallen off — that cut must have been giving him trouble. But the nipper kept on dancing until he wobbled a bit and tripped over Patch. He fell flat on the ground and lay there shaking cos he was upset. He couldn't help it. It was an accident. I rushed over to help him.

A man called out, 'What's the matter with the boy?'

Then somebody said, 'He has the shaking fever. I saw it once in India. It's highly contagious. No one touch him!'

There were shrieks as people panicked and began to hurry away. Some fled, holding handkerchiefs to their noses, leaving me to pick up the nipper who was sobbing his little heart out, clinging to Patch.

In just a few minutes the area in front of the Lyceum was empty except for the flower sellers who were picking up their baskets ready to leave. We had done our best but we hadn't earned a single penny. Not a farthing. I picked Alfie up and set him onto a low wall.

Eliza inspected his foot and wiped away the blood with the edge of her petticoat. 'It don't look good, do it, Sam?' she said. 'It's all pink and swollen, look. He needs another bandage on it before it gets worse.'

We were bending over looking at Alfie's cut when, like some magic trick at the music hall, a hand appeared holding a fine a silk handkerchief. We looked up and gawped. A gentleman of middle years with dark curly hair and a black cape over his suit was standing in front of us. He had a fine gold watch chain dangling from a scarlet waistcoat.

'Tie this round his foot,' the gentleman said and Eliza took the handkerchief.

'Thank you, sir,' she replied, her voice trembling as she stared at him. We weren't used to toffs speaking to us, see.

You could tell he wasn't no ordinary man. I wondered if he was Prince Albert. But the queen wasn't with him and I didn't like to ask.

Eliza wrapped the handkerchief around the cut, all the while keeping her head down – embarrassed, I suppose. She didn't say a word.

The man sat on the wall next to Alfie and lit a cigar. 'You dance very well, little fellow,' he said. 'It's no shame if you trip up sometimes. I have a son of your age called Francis and he is forever falling over.'

Alfie hung his head. 'I don't never trip normally,' he said, wiping a tear from his cheek. 'It's my foot, see. It hurts bad.'

The man drew on his cigar then glanced across at two other toffs who were standing not far away.

'Talfourd! Forster! Come and introduce yourselves to these fine young people.'

The men stepped forward, smiling and shook hands with us like we were real toffs. And they didn't seem worried about catching a disease.

'This young man has cut his foot and I believe he is in need of a pair of shoes,' said the man with the dark curls. 'Can we oblige him, gentlemen?'

The three of 'em felt inside their jackets and pulled out more coins than I'd ever seen I my life.

'Thank you, sirs,' I said, putting the money into my jacket pocket. 'I'll make sure Alfie gets a pair. I'm much obliged.'

'That's very good of you, I'm sure,' said Eliza, 'but we ain't beggars, sir. I'll sing a song in exchange for your payment.'

One of the men frowned and shook his head. 'We should be going, Charles. This wind is bitterly cold.'

Alfie looked up at him. 'Patch can dance too,' he said. 'Don't you want to watch him?'

The man with the curly hair laughed. 'The wind is nothing, Talfourd! Sit and watch these splendid young people.'

'And the dog,' insisted Alfie.

The man smiled and nodded. 'I want to see your dog, of course.' Then he turned to Eliza. 'Can you sing "The Ivy Green" child?' he asked.

Eliza grinned. 'I know it well, sir. Is it your favourite?'

One of the toffs laughed and said, 'He wrote it, young lady.'

Well, I hadn't never met a man who wrote a song before. Eliza beamed and started to sing while the gents settled themselves on a low wall to listen.

They seemed ever so pleased and when she'd finished they clapped and cheered. Then they stood up and wished us farewell.

'Thank you, sir,' I said to the man with the curly hair. 'Did you really write that song?'

He drew on his cigar and nodded. 'I did indeed.'

'One day, I'd like to write a song,' I said. 'Or even a book. I like reading, sir.'

The man smiled at me. 'I think you would do well, my boy. May good fortune go with you.' Then the three of them walked away towards the Strand.

We were counting the money when, out of nowhere, Joe Bolly arrived.

'Done all right, have yer?' he said. 'How much you got?'

'Nearly ten bob,' I told him.

'I didn't do so bad myself,' he said and pulled out three silk handkerchiefs and a pocket watch.

We stared open-mouthed.

'Did them toffs give 'em to yer?' asked Alfie.

'I helped myself,' said Joe. 'That's the best way to do it, see.' And he burst out laughing.

Eliza looked shocked. 'Are you a dipper?'

He frowned. 'It's a living, ain't it? Anyway, where did that silk handkerchief come from?' He was pointing at Alfie's foot. 'A family heirloom was it?'

'No,' I said. 'A cove with curly hair gave it us. He was a real toff. He just came out of the theatre.'

'I know the one,' Joe said. 'I saw him walking away. That's Mister Charles Dickens, that is. He's always good for a few bob if you look poor enough.'

'Charles Dickens?' I said. 'Him what wrote *Oliver Twist*?'

'That's him. You can read, can yer?' he sneered.

'It's our pa's book. He used to read it to us,' said Eliza. 'It's exciting.'

'I didn't like the bit about the undertaker,' said Alfie. 'It was scary.'

Joe didn't seem interested. I thought maybe he couldn't read, see, but being a cocky sort of a lad, he didn't like to admit it.

When we were ready to go, I went to pick up Alfie. But Joe

said, 'Give him here. I'll carry the little un for a bit.' He lifted
Alfie onto his shoulders and we set off. 'Where are you going?'

'Back to Devil's Acre,' I said. 'We'll stay the night by the
Abbey.'

'Not spending your money on lodgings then?'

'No,' said Eliza. 'We'll buy a baked potato, but we'll save the
rest. We're going to find our grandpa, see.'

'He's rich,' said Alfie. 'He lives in a big house and he'll look
after us.'

'You're lucky, ain't yer? Wish I had a rich grandpa, little 'un.'

Halfway down the Strand, we stopped to buy hot potatoes.

'Get one for Patch, Sam,' said Alfie, 'and Joe, too. It's only
fair.'

'Course I will, nipper. You've been a good friend, Joe.
Thank you.'

We all had a potato. They were big ones – crisp on the
outside and soft in the middle – and they filled our empty
bellies very nicely.

At the end of the Strand where the road forked, Joe set
Alfie down on the pavement.

'I'm going this way,' he said, pointing down Cockspur
Street. 'Good luck, matey. I hope you finds your grandpa.' He
grinned and patted me on the back and he held Eliza's hand
and kissed it as if she was a princess. Then he pretended to
punch Alfie on the chest and jumped around like a boxer
before lifting him up onto my shoulders.

We all laughed at his antics and when he crossed the street
and headed home we were sorry to see him go.

Twenty

The night at the abbey

By the time we reached Devil's Acre, the wind was bitterly cold and rain was falling. The narrow streets were dark but we knew our way around and when we turned into Tufton Street and walked past the grand windows of Wippoll & Co, we knew we were very near Westminster Abbey.

The moon came out and lit up the abbey walls making it look like a great black mountain.

'It feels scary, don't it, Sam?' said Eliza, clinging onto my arm.

'If we stay together,' I said, 'we'll be fine.' And we walked along the sides of the abbey where there were places perfect for sheltering. Each one of 'em could hold twenty or thirty people – if you didn't mind squashing up together. There was a roof over your head and some shelter from the wind.

We looked for some time and found a space at last. It was smaller than the rest – just big enough for the three of us – but it was dry and sheltered. We were about to settle down when I saw something move in the dark shadow. I squinted to see what it was when suddenly a face appeared in a patch of moonlight and wild eyes glared at us.

'This is my place,' a voice growled and a hand grabbed hold of Alfie who screamed out loud.

Patch started barking and went to bite the man hidden in the shadows. But a great boot kicked out and sent the poor dog up into the air, landing with a thud.

'We're goin' mister,' I said, grabbing hold of Alfie. 'We didn't know you was there. Honest.'

The man grunted and settled down while Eliza picked up the dog and we hurried away.

It seemed that all the best spots were taken. People were curled up on the ground, wrapping their arms round bundles that held anything they owned, afraid they might be stolen while they slept.

At last we found an empty spot at the far end and settled down with Alfie in the middle. He wasn't hurt. He was more upset about Patch.

'That was a horrible man,' he said, lifting Patch onto his lap. 'And you're a brave dog, ain't yer?' And he hugged the pup who seemed none the worse for his kicking.

Eliza put her arms round Alfie and pulled him close. 'It was exciting, singing outside the theatre, weren't it?' she said. 'And what about meeting Mister Dickens like that?'

I pulled Pa's copy of *Oliver Twist* out of my pocket and stared at it – although it was so dark in our corner that I couldn't see to read. 'I can't believe that gent wrote our book. But maybe one day I'll write something like this, eh? Who knows?'

'What will we do tomorrow?' asked Alfie. 'Will we go to Grandpa's house?'

'Tomorrow we'll go to the pawn shop and buy the box,' said Eliza. 'Then we'll get you a fine pair of boots just like we promised Mister Dickens.'

Alfie smiled. 'If there's some money left, can you and Sam have boots too?' Alfie always liked things to be fair.

'Course we can,' I said.

He leaned against the abbey wall and snuggled between Eliza and me, warm as toast with Patch on his lap. His eyelids soon drooped and his head lolled against my shoulder.

When Eliza was sure he was asleep, she whispered, 'It'll be all right, won't it, Sam? We'll get the box, won't we? I want to find Grandpa.'

'Course we will, Eliza,' I said, feeling drowsy. 'Go to sleep. We've got plenty of money to buy the box.' And I patted my jacket pocket.

But instead of feeling the bulge of the coins, the pocket was flat. Suddenly I was wide awake and a cold shiver ran down my spine. I pushed my hand inside, hoping to feel the money. But it was gone. All of it. Could it be in the other pocket? I thought. No. There was a hole in that one and I only kept the book in it. Anything smaller would drop out.

I had to face it. The money had been stolen.

What now? Should I tell Eliza or should I wait till morning?

Twenty-One
Eliza's plan

I knew where the money was for sure. It was in Joe Bolly's pocket. He was a dipper. A good one. He had probably been thieving since he could walk.

I thought back on what had happened. When he slapped me on the back he must have slipped his hand into my pocket. Some friend! I'd been taken in by him all right. What a fool I was. I'd lost the money and let my family down.

All that night I sat with my knees under my chin, worrying. Eliza and Alfie slept soundly and, even when Patch growled at someone passing by, they never woke. I tried to think what we should do next. But I could only see a grim future, earning barely enough for food. Spending nights in cold shelters. That was our future. Or worse – we'd end up in the workhouse.

As it grew light that morning, the sky was heavy with rain. I waited for Eliza to open her eyes and then I told her the money was gone.

'No!' she said in a low voice so as not to wake Alfie. Then she sat up straight, staring into space as a tear spilled onto her cheek.

'Sorry, Eliza,' I said. 'I never saw him take it.'

I felt ashamed and stupid. I couldn't look at her. It had been my fault.

'Everything's going from bad to worse,' I said. 'We can't buy the box now. We're done for.'

'No we ain't,' she said, trying to smile. 'I can always sing and Alfie can dance when his foot's better. We'll have crowds of people watching and we'll earn enough in a day or two.'

I shook my head. 'It's raining and it's cold,' I said, looking up at the black clouds. 'You can't go singing in the streets. Nobody will stop and listen to you on a day like this. If we can't buy the box today, they might sell it.'

'Right then,' she said, putting on a brave face. 'We'll walk over to Tothill Street and ask the pawnbroker ever so nicely if he'll give us the letters out of the box. I'm sure he will. Then at least we'll have Grandpa's address and we can go and find him.'

Alfie stirred and opened his eyes. 'Our grandfather's rich, ain't he?' he said, snuggling up to Eliza. 'He'll look after us, won't he?' And he fell asleep again.

I didn't think much of Eliza's plan. 'Pawnbrokers are rogues,' I whispered. 'Don't you know they buy stolen goods for next to nothing? Then they sell 'em dear.' I sighed. 'A pawnbroker won't give you so much as a dead fly.'

'And what if he ain't a rogue? What if he don't want them letters? I've never heard of anyone buying letters. Nobody will pay good money for letters writ for somebody else, will they?'

I shook my head. 'It won't work, Eliza. What's the point, eh?'

But she was determined. She shook Alfie's arm. 'Wake up, nipper,' she said. 'We're going to see the pawnbroker.'

'I'm tired,' he moaned and turned over.

'Then I'll go myself and leave you two behind.'

With that, she got to her feet and marched off in the direction of Tothill Street.

Twenty-Two

The pawnbroker's shop

The pawnbroker's shop was not far from the abbey. I ran after Eliza with Alfie riding piggyback.

Tothill Street was long, with crumbling houses on either side. The pawnbroker's was halfway along it and there were three balls hanging over the door so that those who couldn't read would know it was a pawnbroker's shop. For those who could read, there was a sign fixed over the window: G SACKMAN PAWNBROKER SINCE 1839.

Eliza knew we'd follow her and she'd spent her time peering into the shop which was lined with shelves and stacked with everything from shoes to walking sticks. By the time Alfie and me had caught up with her, she'd spotted the silver box.

'It's there,' she squealed, pointing to a high shelf. Finally, some luck! We pressed our noses to the window and stared through the dirty glass. 'Come on!' she said. 'Let's go and get it.'

I still wasn't sure this was a good idea but Eliza stepped into the shop holding Alfie's hand. A little brass bell fixed to the door made a tinkling noise. I followed behind half-heartedly. The shop was small and square. In the middle was a table, acting as a counter, and behind it was a small lady, tidily dressed in grey with brown hair pulled back off her face. She was sitting in a comfy armchair knitting a red woolly jumper and I guessed she must be the pawnbroker's wife. As we walked in, she glanced up from her knitting, not looking at all pleased to see children like us in her shop – young uns in need of a good meal, a wash and a pair of shoes.

She put her knitting on the table and stared at Eliza. 'Has your pa sent you?' she asked. 'Have you got something to show me?'

Eliza stepped closer. 'We was wanting to see Mister Sackman,' she said in a whisper. 'We got something to ask him.'

The woman shrugged. 'He's out on business and won't be back until midday. Have you got something to sell? I'll give you a fair price for it.'

'We ain't got nothing to sell,' Alfie butted in. 'We ain't got no money, but you've got our ma's box and we want to go and find our grandpa and we're taking my dog with us and we're going to be rich.'

Missus Sackman puffed out her cheeks looking puzzled and confused. She hadn't understood a word Alfie had said. I stepped forward to explain.

But before I could, the pawnbroker's wife leaned forward and blinked. 'It's you,' she said. 'It is, isn't it? It's you!'

I stared back and wondered if I'd seen her before. Then she stood up and I saw she was no taller than Eliza. I suddenly recognised her – she was the customer in Missus Abdale's pie shop.

'You was the lad what found my necklace,' she said.

I nodded. 'Yes, I did.'

'Then I'm very pleased to meet you again, young man,' she said, grabbing hold of my hand and shaking it so heartily that I feared it would drop off. 'I tell you, I was that scared when you came running after me. I thought you was some kind of villain. And when you gave me my necklace, I didn't know what to say.' Then she clapped her hands together and burst out laughing.

Alfie pushed in between us. 'It was your necklace, missus. It was only fair you should have it back.'

Missus Sackman smiled at him. 'Not many people around these parts would think like that, little un. There are more thieves than honest men, I'm thinking.' She looked at me again. 'Now tell me your name, young man.'

'It's Sam Pargeter, missus, and this is my sister Eliza and the nipper is Alfie.'

'Well, you're all very welcome. That necklace was special, see. My son gave it to me before he went away to sea. I would have been mighty upset if I'd lost it.' She sat down again and leaned on the table. 'Now then, tell me what I can do for you.'

'All we want,' I said, pointing to the top shelf, 'is the letters inside that box up there. We ain't got no money but we was wondering if we could have 'em? . . . Please.'

'Can we?' asked Eliza.

'Can we? Can we?' begged Alfie, jumping up and down with Patch in his arms. 'Please will you let us?'

Missus Sackman held up her hands. 'Why would you want letters? Have you had any schooling? Can you read?'

'I can,' I said. 'And Eliza, too. Pa taught us. There's a letter to our grandpa, see, and it's got his address on the front. We can't find him without the address.'

'He's rich,' said Alfie, 'and he's going to look after us. He's kind, ain't he, Eliza? And he'll look after Patch even though he only walks on three legs.'

Eliza gave him one of her warning looks and pressed her fingers to her lips.

Missus Sackman slapped her hand on the table. 'Of course you can have the letters, my dears. My husband's a good man. He won't have no objections.'

She got up to fetch the silver box but, being quite a short woman, she couldn't reach to top shelf. So she stood on a stool, lifted the box down and put it on the counter.

'Here it is, my dears. Go on. You open it.'

We lifted the lid, hoping the letters would still be there. When we peered inside, I couldn't stop myself from shouting out, 'Lawks! There they are. All three of 'em.'

I was that excited, I spread them out on the table just so I could look at them.

'These two written was written by Pa,' I explained, pointing to each one. 'He sent them to Ma. Our Aunt Maud wrote this one to Grandpa. His address is there, see. That's where we're going.'

'He's rich,' Alfie added again.

Missus Sackman smiled. 'You take them letters with my

blessing,' she said. 'Mister Sackman won't mind. They ain't worth nothing to nobody but you. Just keep 'em safe, eh? I don't want you losing 'em, do I?' And she picked them up and handed them to me.

Eliza was that pleased, she flung her arms round Missus Sackman's neck. 'Oh, thank you, thank you,' she said and kissed her on the cheek.

The pawnbroker's wife blushed but you could tell she didn't mind really. 'Where's your ma now, my loves?' she asked.

'Gone to heaven,' said Alfie.

'And your pa?'

'He went to foreign parts and got swallowed up by one of them wild animals,' he said.

Eliza grabbed his hand. 'We're not sure, Missus Sackman. He ain't come back.'

'And what about your aunt? Her what wrote the letter. Where's she?'

'Run off!' Alfie bawled. 'She climbed out of the window, she did. Now we ain't got nobody to look after us.'

After that, I told her everything – I even the bit about Joe Bolly.

Missus Sackman listened and when I'd finished, she took a handkerchief from her apron pocket, wiped her eyes and blew her nose until it turned red.

'Well, you have had a bad time of it,' she said. 'Perhaps I can tempt you with something to eat, seeing as how I've got some fine sausages in the back room. They're just waiting for hungry children to come along.'

At the mention of food, our mouths began to water. We followed the pawnbroker's wife through a door which led into a room where the Sackmans lived. Straight away, Missus Sackman put a huge frying pan onto the fire and filled it with plump pork sausages which sizzled away until they turned a delicious shade of brown and were ready to eat.

'Settle yourselves down, my loves,' said Missus Sackman, pointing to the chairs around a table. Then she reached three plates off a shelf, shared out the sausages and set them in front of us. Patch, who was sitting by Alfie's chair, looked up longingly.

'I expect he's hungry too, ain't he?' asked Missus Sackman.

Alfie, his mouth full of sausage, nodded. So the pawnbroker's wife went in search of meat scraps and bread which she put in a dish.

We soon polished off the sausages and wiped our plates clean with a good chunk of bread. And once my belly was full, I felt sleepy. I hadn't slept the night before what with worrying about the money, so it was no surprise that I started to nod off. Eliza was the same, and Alfie too. We all folded our arms onto the table, rested our heads on them and closed our eyes. Even Patch, after licking his dish clean, curled up on the rug.

Missus Sackman fetched her knitting and settled in an armchair by the fire, keeping an eye on us in a motherly kind of way until the little brass bell attached to the front door tinkled. Someone had come into the shop.

Twenty-Three

Murder!

At the tinkling of the bell, we lifted our heads and opened our eyes. Patch sat up and twitched his ears.

'You stay by the fire, my dears,' said Missus Sackman as she got up out of her chair. 'I'll go and see to the customer.'

Patch was so grateful for the food, she had given him, he would have followed Missus Sackman anywhere — so he trotted after her into the shop.

We all put our heads down again and went back to sleep. I'd only just dozed off again when I was jerked awake. Patch was barking and Missus Sackman was screaming. 'No! Stop! Help! Oh, help!'

And then there was a noise that sounded scarily like a gun.

We all jumped up and raced into the shop where we found Missus Sackman flapping her hands and going all hysterical. She was pointing to a man sprawled on the floor, moaning and groaning while Patch attacked his leg. It was a horrible sight. Blood was oozing everywhere.

'Pull him off me!' the man begged.

But Missus Sackman kept yelling, 'Murder! Thief! Get the villain out of my shop! Out, out, out! Heaven help us!' Then she suddenly stopped. The colour drained from her face, her knees buckled under her and she fell to the floor.

Eliza went to help her while I forced Patch to let go of the intruder who was howling in agony. Somehow he scrambled to his feet and headed out of the shop, dragging his injured leg.

'Good riddance!' I shouted and turned the key in the lock, in case he came back.

I hurried over to lift poor Missus Sackman off the floor. She was lying there, having fainted clean away. Her eyes were closed and she looked pale as paper.

'We'll have to get her onto the chair,' I said and between Eliza and me, we manage to lift her.

While we were settling Missus Sackman, Alfie was comforting Patch who was over-excited following his brave attack on the thief. The nipper was about to take the dog into the back room when he spotted something under the table.

'It's a gun, Sam,' he said and picked it up. 'That man must have dropped it...I ain't seen a real gun before.'

'Put it down, Alfie,' I said just as there was a terrible banging at the shop door. I looked up and saw a crowd of neighbours, who must have heard the gun shot and the screaming, trying to get in. I left Missus Sackman's side, to unlock the door but instead of waiting for me to do it, they put their shoulders to the door and forced it open.

'Caught you red-handed, you little varmint!' bellowed a white-haired man who grabbed hold of Alfie and snatched the gun out of his hand.

'Leave my brother alone,' I yelled. 'He—'

'He what?' the man shouted. 'Likes to fire guns, does he?'

Then a woman, seeing Missus Sackman lifeless in the chair began to scream. 'Oh, look they've killed her. She's dead, she is. Dead!'

Before we could say anything, four men leaped on Eliza and me and dragged us away. Patch set off barking again and snapping at their heels.

'Get that dog out of here!' someone shouted and a man delivered a savage kick which sent Patch yelping and flying through the open door into the street.

Missus Sackman was carried away into the back room while the three of us were surrounded by the terrifying neighbours who kept yelling, 'Murderers! You killed Missus Sackman!'

'We ain't killed nobody,' Eliza protested. 'We was just—'

'Little liar,' shouted a woman. 'We heard the gun go off, we did.'

One of the men held his clenched his fist in my face. 'We're a respectable neighbourhood, see. I'll give you a right thrashing,' he growled and I thought I was for it until somebody else called, 'My brother's gone to fetch the constable. He'll soon have 'em locked up.'

My knees turned to jelly while everybody shouted and hollered. I could hardly hear myself think. Then a man rushed into the shop, red in the face and obviously in a real panic. This was not the constable. It turned out to be Mister Sackman, the pawnbroker, who had been told about the shooting and had run all the way from his meeting at the Boar's Head.

'Where's my missus?' he demanded, his eyes darting around the room. 'Where is she?'

The neighbours looked glum and pointed to the door that led to the parlour. He was about to push his way through the crowd when he suddenly spotted the three of us.

'Lawks! Are these the scoundrels what killed my Nellie?'

When the people of Tothill Street said that we were, he let out a howl of rage and raised his hand to attack me, being the oldest. Luckily somebody caught hold of him before he could strike.

He was shaking with anger. 'Get them to the magistrate,' he roared, 'or I'll murder the little blighters myself.'

Just as the pawnbroker stormed off into the back room, the shop door opened and a constable marched in. He was taller than any of the other men on account of his top hat, which was so high he looked like a giant. His cheeks were covered with bushy black whiskers so scary that Alfie howled louder than ever and ran to Eliza, clinging to her waist.

'Where are the culprits?' the constable shouted as he marched into the shop waving his truncheon.

'Over here,' called a neighbour. 'These three beggars have committed a murder. Poor Missus Sackman's body is in the parlour.'

After that, everybody started yelling and pointing at us as if we were criminals. Alfie was in floods of tears and kept shrieking, 'Where's Patch? Where's Patch?' And I was just as terrified, not knowing what was going to happen us. Even when I tried to explain, no one would listen. They were all talking at once. The noise was deafening.

But when the constable held up his hand and shouted, 'Silence!' everybody stopped. Even Alfie, who just stared at the policeman in shock.

'So there's been a murder, has there?' he said, picking up the gun. 'Then I take it that these 'ere ruffians are the criminals what broke into the shop and fired the gun at Missus Sackman?'

'Aye,' one called. 'Ten minutes since. They shot Missus Sackman in cold blood.'

'No, we—' I started.

But the constable frowned and gave me a warning look. Then he started to examine the gun. 'Mmm,' he said. 'A fine gun. An Adams revolver.'

The crowd seemed very impressed that he knew all about firearms, except for the man with the white hair who I'd heard someone call Mister Gumble. 'Get on with it, man. Never mind the gun. Arrest the scoundrels. We shan't feel safe in our beds until they're behind bars.'

The constable tucked his truncheon into a pocket at the back of his long blue coat. 'I'll take them to the police station,' he said as he pulled out a pair of handcuffs.

'You should take 'em to the beak,' said Mister Gumble. 'See what he's got to say.'

'Steady, man,' said the constable. 'They'll be safe enough in a cell until they go for trial.'

The angry crowd roared. 'String 'em up! The sooner the better!'

'Leave us alone!' I yelled for the hundredth time. 'We ain't done nothing.' But it didn't make no difference. They didn't listen.

The policeman began to look nervous as more people crowded into the shop and shouted their opinions about what to do with us. In the end, he grabbed hold of me and fixed the handcuffs on my wrists which hurt real bad.

'Now then,' he called to the crowd. 'I've cuffed the oldest one. But I've only got the one pair. Who'll volunteer to take the wench and the little lad?'

There was a roar as people pushed forward to snatch hold of them.

'Just go with these people!' I shouted to Eliza and Alfie. 'We'll find someone who'll listen to us at the police station.'

In spite of Eliza screaming and thrashing about, they managed to grab her and soon we were all bundled through the door, followed by the angry mob who were determined to see us punished.

Twenty-Four
The mob

It was horrible. The news of the shooting spread and the crowd of neighbours soon swelled into a rabble. The constable walked in front still holding onto me. Mister Gumble gripped Eliza's arm while Alfie was being pulled along by a fierce-looking man with bushy black eyebrows.

I felt frightened all right. But I felt angry too. What right had these people to manhandle us like this? Why wouldn't they listen to what we had to say?

The mob followed close behind, pushing and yelling and shaking their fists. They shouted so loud that the noise echoed round us as we were dragged up King Street towards the police station. The mob could string us up from a lamppost and nobody would stop them. Scared stiff, we were. And who could blame us? If we were found guilty of murder, we'd be hanged for certain.

When the police station came into view, I trembled at the sight of it and dug my heels into the ground and struggled again to free myself. But it was no good. I was dragged the last few yards and Alfie's cries grew louder as we got nearer. The worst thing was, I couldn't do nothing to help him.

A policeman, with a large belly and a black moustache, came running out of the station, followed by six others. 'What's going on, Tribbett?' he shouted. 'What's happening? Is it a riot?'

Constable Tribbett was panting like a dog by then. 'Murder, sergeant,' he gasped. 'Caught 'em red-handed. This mob is out for their blood, I tell you.'

'Bring 'em in quick before it gets out of hand,' barked the sergeant and he marched inside, his back straight as a ramrod. The constable followed with the three of us, Mister Gumble and the man with the bushy eyebrows. Meanwhile the other policemen stayed out in the street, trying to keep order and refusing to let anyone else go inside.

Once the sergeant, whose name I learned was Whither-spoon, was settled behind his desk. He took up his pencil and prepared to take notes. 'Now,' he said. 'Tell me what this is all about.'

'It's like this, sergeant...' and Constable Tribbett described what he had seen – or thought he'd seen – in the pawnbroker's shop. He told how he had tackled the criminals (us) and how poor Missus Sackman was in the back room, having been shot in the chest by one of our gang (Alfie).

'No!' Eliza protested. 'It weren't like that. We was helping her.'

'Alfie didn't use that gun,' I said. 'He just picked it up. There was a man in the shop, see, and he—'

But before I could say more, the sergeant, gripped his desk and leaned forward, as red-faced as a holly berry. 'Silence!' he shouted. 'Keep your traps shut, you little scoundrels, or I'll

130

put you down below.' Then he turned to Constable Tribbett. 'Do we have any witnesses?'

Immediately, Mister Gumble stepped forward. 'I am a witness,' he said, puffing out his chest, all important like. 'I saw it all. It was terrible, your honour.' He took off his cap and bowed his head as if he were in front of the queen. 'When I went into the shop, this 'ere lad' – he pointed at me – 'and the wench were standing over poor Missus Sackman in a very suspicious manner. And that there little un,' he said, wagging his finger at Alfie, 'he had just shot her. He was still holding the gun. I saw it myself.'

'No he didn't shoot—'

'Quiet!' yelled the sergeant.

Then the constable shook me by the collar. 'This one's the leader.' He pushed me forward. 'They're a gang of real villains, mark my words. A family of low lifes from Devil's Acre. You know the type, serge.'

'I do indeed,' said Sergeant Whitherspoon, licking the lead in his pencil before starting to write.

'Name?' he said, looking at me cos I was nearest.

'I'm Sam Pargeter...but I ain't no criminal.'

Constable Tribbett swiped me across the head with the back of his hand. 'Just answer the question, lad.'

'Don't you hit my brother,' shouted Eliza. 'We didn't do nothing. But we know who did.'

'We do,' I said. 'Why won't you listen to us?'

'Awwww!' wailed Alfie. 'We didn't do nothing. We didn't do nothing. It wasn't us.'

The sergeant slammed his pencil on the desk and glared. 'Right. I've had enough of all this racket. Take 'em down and lock 'em up. Put 'em in separate cells. Let 'em stew.'

'No!' yelled Eliza, struggling to free herself while Alfie set up screeching and screaming fit to burst your eardrums. Then I elbowed Constable Tribbett in the belly. I'm sorry if I hurt him. He was only doing his job, but nobody would listen, see.

By then there was such a uproar that two more policemen rushed in from the street and helped to drag the three of us down a flight of steps which led down to the cells. It was ever so dark – lit by a single candle. The stone floor was slippery and slimy and there was a terrible stink. Enough to make you throw up. Worse than the privy behind the lodging house.

'There's only one cell empty,' said the constable. 'They'll have to go in the same one.'

Tribbett pushed the cell door but it was slow to open on account of its rusty hinges. We were shoved inside, and when he slammed it shut and locked it, an icy shiver ran down my spine. The cell was bleak and cold with a blanket dumped on the floor and a tin bucket in the corner.

'How long will we be here?' I shouted through the grille as the policemen walked away.

'You've got a few days before you go before the magistrate,' he called. 'So get used to your new living quarters.'

'Aye,' laughed another constable. 'Then you can say goodbye to your necks. You'll be for the drop.'

'What's "the drop"?' asked Alfie but the police didn't answer and there was no way I was going to tell him we might be hanged.

When they'd gone, Alfie curled up on the floor, shaking and a sobbing and calling for Ma. Eliza put her arms round him and rocked him. But nothing made him feel better. I even suggested we sang some songs but that didn't help. He just cried and cried.

'Stow it, will yer?' a rough voice boomed from the next cell. 'That din is making me head split open.'

'He's only six, mister,' I called back, 'and he ain't got no mother.'

There was an outbreak of laughing and guffawing from the other cells.

'No mother, eh?' someone shouted. 'Just as well. She wouldn't want to see her little darlin's swinging from a rope, would she?'

Alfie was already hysterical with fear, but when Ma was mentioned he suddenly flew into a rage. 'You leave my ma out of it!' he yelled. 'I didn't do nothin'! They said I fired that gun but I didn't. I didn't!'

'No, he didn't, mister,' said Eliza. 'But nobody listens to us. It's a wicked shame. We was helping this lady, see, and—'

'Shut it, missy. I got worries of me own. Us costermongers are always up in front of the beak.'

'Quite right too,' somebody called from another cell.

'Said I'd stolen the fish on me cart. But it weren't true.'

'You costermongers are no better than thieves,' said

another voice. 'Expect you'll get sent to Australia.'

Then a fourth voice said, 'They say it's burning hot down there. There's cholera about. You won't last long.'

'Stow it, you old soaker!' roared the costermonger.

'You stall your mug,' yelled someone else. 'You tell whackers, you do.'

'If I ever get my hands on you...'

On and on they went. They roared and cursed each other. They banged and rattled at the doors making such a deafening din that we crouched in a corner, covering our ears to shut it out.

When they finally quietened down, I pulled the letters from my pocket.

'Which shall I read first, nipper?' I said to cheer him up.

Alfie brushed the tears from him cheeks. 'Pa's,' he said. 'The one where he says how much he misses us.'

In a quiet voice so the others wouldn't hear, I read Pa's letters and then I read Aunt Maud's letter to Grandpa.

'What will Grandpa's house be like, do you think?' asked Alfie.

Eliza hugged him. 'I think it'll be the most splendiferous house in England,' she said. 'There'll be lots of rooms and food every day and fields to play in.'

And that seemed to please him no end.

As for me, I wondered how long we would be in this rotten hole. I wanted to get out. But what would happen then? Would it be the magistrate or the hangman?

Twenty-Five

A friendly face

Since Aunt Maud and Uncle Bert had done a runner, things had gone from bad to worse. We'd been left on our own in Devil's Acre and now we were locked up as common criminals, accused of murder.

We were there all day in the cell without seeing anybody. Only hearing the shouts and the arguments of the other prisoners. Coarse men with coarse language. Ma would have been shocked we should hear such things.

The day seemed endless and I was running out of ways to cheer up the others. Then I heard footsteps coming down the steps.

'Oi, oi!' yelled one of the men. 'Is that Missus Whitherspoon I hear? Brought us our supper, have yer?'

The other men started yelling then, but she shouted back at them with a voice like a foghorn. 'Quiet, you lot,' she bellowed, 'or you'll have none.'

It did the trick. The men stopped their calling and Missus Whitherspoon's face appeared at the bars of our cell door. I can't tell you how glad I was to see her. She was an angel, that's what I thought. An angel with a round face and a wobbly chin.

'I'm Missus Whitherspoon,' she said. 'My husband, Sergeant Whitherspoon, said he's got some varmints in the cell tonight.'

'We're not varmints,' Eliza shouted. 'We're not. Honest.'

'Well what you done is no concern of mine,' she said. 'I'm just the cook. If you want some supper I'll bring you something.'

At this, the men in the other cells set up such a shouting and a yelling.

'Hey, missus, don't forget us.'

'I'll have a big bowl o' your stew, missus.'

'Don't feed 'em, Missus W. They're just low life. We'll have their share.'

Missus Whitherspoon didn't say a word until the din had died down. Then she said, 'Mind your manners or you'll get a crust of bread and nothing more.' There were loud groans. 'Say another word and you'll go without your supper.'

'But I'm starving.'

'Ah, ah, ah,' she snapped. 'Another word, I said.'

Obviously thinking they would have to go without food, they decided that it was best to keep quiet although, being used to shouting and bawling, they must have found it hard.

'Now,' she called to us through the bars. 'Would the two of you like some beef stew?'

'Yes, please,' said Eliza, 'and Alfie too. Don't forget him.'

Missus W stretched up on tip toe. 'Where's Alfie?'

'I'm Alfie,' he said, stepping out from behind me. His eyes were red and swollen from crying and he hardly lifted his chin to look up at the sergeant's wife.

'Oh my lawd!' she said. 'He's hardly more than a baby.'

'He's six,' I said.

Suddenly Missus Whitherspoon's eyes filled with tears. 'Well, I never,' she said with a sniff. 'Just like my Ernest.' She wiped her eyes with the back of her hand. 'Six years old he was with big blue eyes. Just the same.'

'Who's Ernest?' asked Alfie.

Missus Whitherspoon shook her head. 'Gone,' she said. 'Gone these four years and I still miss him.' For a minute she looked sad just like Ma when she thought about little Henry. But she suddenly pulled herself together and said, 'So you'd like something to eat then?'

'Yes, thanks, Missus Whitherspoon,' I said. 'We ain't had nothing since Missus Sackman gave us sausages this morning.'

'Who's Missus Sackman?'

'She's the lady we're supposed to have murdered.'

'You went and killed her after she was good enough to feed you?'

'But we didn't kill her,' insisted Eliza squeezing next to me. 'It was a cove who came into the shop with a gun.'

'Ain't nobody listens to us, Missus Whitherspoon,' I said.

'And why's that?'

'Because we're kids,' Eliza replied. 'They won't take no notice of us.'

The sergeant's wife put her hand to her cheek. She was probably wondering whether we'd told her the truth. Perhaps we'd murdered Missus Sackman. Perhaps we hadn't. How could she be sure?

Whatever she had decided, she said, 'That's enough chat. I'll go and fetch the stew.'

'Aye. Get a move on, missus,' shouted the man from the far cell. 'Me belly's rumblin' fit to wake the dead.'

'Don't you give me orders,' she snapped at him. 'You'll think yourself lucky if there's a spoonful left for you.'

She marched off up the steps and when she came back half an hour later, she was carrying tin plates, some pieces of bread and a large pan of stew which gave off a smell good enough to send you into a swoon.

'You enjoy that,' Missus Whitherspoon said as she pushed the plates of stew under the door. We picked them up, warming our hands under the plates for the cell was cold and damp.

'Is that good?' she called out as we spooned the stew into our mouths.

'Mmmmm,' said Alfie. 'Golopshus!' And we heard her chuckle.

'Thanks, Missus Whitherspoon,' I said between mouthfuls.

'You're a crack cook, Missus Whitherspoon,' said Eliza. 'Thank you.'

The sergeant's wife waited outside the door for the empty plates.

'You two big uns take care of your brother,' said Missus W as she gathered up the plates and stacked them in a pile. 'I'll see you in the morning. If you're innocent, like you says you is, I'm sure the truth will out. Sleep tight and don't you worry about a thing – especially them rats. They won't do you no harm. They're God's creatures when all's said and done.'

We sat on the cold floor. I wrapped my arms round Alfie and said, 'Sing to us, Eliza.' She sang 'Twinkle Twinkle Little Star' in the quietest voice while I rocked Alfie backwards and forwards. And when he fell asleep, I closed my eyes too, hoping Missus W was right and someone would come soon and save us.

Twenty-Six

The interview room

The next morning, in cell number four at King Street police station, we were feeling doomed. The men in the other cells kept calling to us, 'You still there, little uns?', 'Not eaten by the rats in the night?' which made Alfie shake with fear. And Eliza and me didn't feel much better – we'd not had more than a couple of winks sleep.

'Don't listen to 'em, Alfie,' I said. 'We'll soon be out of here.' It was probably a lie but I had to cheer him up somehow.

Missus Whitherspoon carried a pan of steaming hot porridge down the stairs, ready to dish out onto tin plates. As she passed ours under the door, I noticed a funny look. She didn't say nothing – but I had a feeling something was up.

It was later that morning that I heard heavy footsteps coming down the stone steps and the face of Constable Tribbett appeared at the door of the cell.

'Somebody wants to see you lot,' he said, turning the key in the lock. 'Come on. Look lively.' And he opened the door.

There was uproar from the men. 'Wot's goin' on? Takin' 'em to the beak, are yer?' And to be honest, I didn't know whether to be glad that we were leaving or scared of where we might be going to.

The constable grabbed hold of my arm. 'You two varmints stay close behind,' he said to Eliza and Alfie, 'or you'll be for it! Do you understand?'

They nodded and the constable dragged me up the steps, my heart pounding while they followed. He took us down a long corridor and stopped outside a door labelled *Interview Room*.

'Mind you behaves yourselves!' he said, giving me a slap across the back of my head. 'Make sure you show some respect to your betters.' And he opened the door and pushed the three of us inside.

You could have knocked me down with a feather! The room was full! What a surprise. Lawks! There was Missus Sackman sitting at a long table looking very pale but very much not dead! And Mister Sackman, was sitting next to her. Missus Whitherspoon was there too, looking very pleased. And opposite them all was Sergeant Whitherspoon with four sharpened pencils laid neatly on the table and a pile of paper.

As if that wasn't enough of a surprise, a blur of black and white came rushing out from under Missus Whitherspoon's skirt and almost bowled Alfie over.

'Patch!' he cried and picked him up and hugged him so tight it's a wonder the little dog wasn't squashed.

'Where did he come from?' I asked Missus Whitherspoon.

'Why, bless him,' she said, 'the little chap was outside the police station. He must have followed you here and been waitin' for you ever since.'

Sergeant Whitherspoon coughed and tapped his pencil on the table. 'Hahummm,' he said. 'I have called this meeting since Missus Sackman came to the Station with important information—'

'Thank the Lord she did, husband,' interrupted his wife. 'And if she hadn't, I believe a terrible injustice would have been done.' She smiled at Missus Sackman and then at the three of us, but I noticed that she saved her biggest smile for Alfie.

'Quite so. Quite so,' said the sergeant. 'But as the sergeant at this 'ere police station I must interview you all and write everything down – even what these young people had to say to Missus Whitherspoon – before I decide what to do with 'em.'

It seemed to me that writing things down was what Sergeant Whitherspoon liked best and he picked up a pencil ready to begin.

'Now, Mister Sackman. If I could hear your account of these shocking events. I shall take some notes.'

Mister Sackman stood up and cleared his throat ready to begin, but the sergeant said, 'No need to stand, sir. Please sit down.'

The pawnbroker settled back into his seat again. 'A neighbour came and fetched me from the Boar's Head where I was ... er ... doing business,' he said. 'He said some varmints had broken into the shop and a young lad had shot my wife.' And he pointed at Alfie. 'When I got back, my missus had been taken into the back room and she wasn't moving or breathing as far as I could tell. So naturally I thought she was dead. She was like that for an hour or more and then suddenly she opened her eyes and asked for a cup of tea. I was that pleased, I went and put the kettle on straight away.' He looked at Missus Sackman and smiled. His wife opened her mouth as if to say something but Mister Sackman patted her on the shoulder and carried on. 'She's a bit shocked. Suffering from a terrible headache, she is. She just needs a bit of rest. But everything's as right as rain, really.'

At that point, Missus Whitherspoon stood up and thumped her fist on the table. 'Right as rain?' she said. 'Oh no, it ain't right as rain, Mister Sackman. Oh no, no, no! There are three children here who was locked up in a cell accused of your wife's murder, and you knew there weren't any murder all along. That can't be right, can it?'

Sergeant Whitherspoon tried to restore order but the pawnbroker jumped to his feet and faced the sergeant's wife. 'Then what was them ruffians doing in my shop in the first place, Missus Whitherspoon? What was they doing with a gun, eh?'

Then I leaped to my feet and yelled, 'We didn't have no gun!' But Constable Tribbett grabbed hold of my arm and sat me down again. 'You stay quiet!' he snapped and poked me in the back.

Mister Sackman was in a terrible temper. 'I promised my wife I'd come here and tell you there weren't no murder. Well, I done that. But mark my words, sergeant, if them children didn't kill my missus, they tried to. They can rot in prison for all I care. They're a bad lot.'

At her husband's outburst, the pawnbroker's wife broke down in tears. 'He won't listen,' she wailed. 'I tried to tell him what happened, but he wouldn't let me.'

Before she could say another word, he put his hand on her shoulder. 'Now, now, Nellie. Calm down. Stay quiet, till you're feeling better.' He looked up at Sergeant Whitherspoon who was writing frantically. 'I think I'd better take her home. She's not at all well.'

'Your wife don't look that bad to me,' the sergeant said. 'If she's got something to say, I'd like to hear it.' He picked up a clean piece of paper and a new pencil ready to take down her statement.

Missus Sackman wiped away her tears and looked up at her husband. 'Don't worry, dear,' she said. 'I know you was just trying to look after me.' Then she turned to the sergeant. 'I've had this terrible headache, see. And he keeps saying I've got to rest and stay quiet. But this morning I couldn't rest no more. I had to come here, see, to make sure these dear children are not accused of my murder.'

'Very well then,' said sergeant, eager to start writing again. 'Tell me what happened yesterday, Missus Sackman. What really happened?'

So the pawnbroker's wife told how the man came into the shop and threatened her with a gun. How Patch bit his leg and the gun went off as the man dropped it. How Eliza and me came to help just before she fainted and banged her head.

'I don't remember nothing after that,' she said.

'But what was them varmints doing in my shop, wife?' Mister Sackman asked. 'Thievin', was they?'

Missus Sackman, who was suddenly looking her old self, sat up straight, colour flushing back into her cheeks. 'No, husband! These children are an honest lot,' she said. 'This lad here found my necklace what I'd dropped the other night over at Missus Abdale's pie shop. Gave it right back, he did. Didn't try to sell it. No! He gave it right back.' She took a deep breath and smoothed her hair from her face. 'They come to the shop looking for their dead mother's letters. They was in a box what you bought off that villain Beddows. Now do you think they were out to murder me?'

The pawnbroker hung his head, his cheeks scarlet from embarrassment. 'Why didn't you tell me?' he said.

Missus Sackman gritted her teeth. 'You wouldn't listen, husband. You wouldn't listen.' She turned and looked at me. 'I'm sorry, Sam.'

After that, the sergeant asked us questions and wrote more notes, which pleased him no end. He took statements from everybody including his own wife. Missus Sackman's had taken five whole pages to explain exactly what had happened. During this time Sergeant Whitherspoon sharpened his pencils three times and almost ran out of paper. When he'd finished, he puffed out his chest and looked exceedingly pleased with himself.

'Right, I think that's all,' he said slapping his pencil on the table. 'According to the law of the land, you three are free to go.' Then he leaned forward and wagged his finger at us. 'Just watch yourselves, you whippersnappers. Don't go getting into any more trouble or you'll have to answer to me.'

That was all very well but I was wondering where we would go now.

As if she could read my mind, Missus Sackman said, 'If you please, you children will come home with me and I'll find you something nice to eat, eh?'

What could be better? 'Yes, please!' said Alfie, and Eliza and me agreed.

We said a long goodbye to Missus Whitherspoon and promised that we'd come back one day. She looked quite upset that we were going – I'm sure she had tears in her eyes – and she gave Alfie a special big hug before we left with the pawnbroker and his wife.

When we got back to the shop Missus Sackman made us very welcome. 'Sit down and make yourselves at home,' she said, putting the kettle on the fire and taking the teapot off the shelf. 'My husband is very sorry for getting you into such trouble, aren't you, dear?'

Mister Sackman looked uncomfortable. I don't think he liked his wife talking about his mistakes, like that. He smiled sheepishly and sat in the armchair nearest to the fire. 'I didn't know nothing,' he said. 'I just wanted what was best for my missus, see.'

'He knows now that you just come here looking for that silver box. Don't you, dear?'

'Yes, dear,' said the pawnbroker. 'I understand now.'

'I've still got the letters that were in it,' I said, pulling one out of my pocket. 'Our grandpa's address is on it. So we know where he lives and we can find him now.'

I held it out for Mister Sackman to see and he leaned forward and screwed up his eyes to read it.

'I can't make out the address,' he said, pointing to the spot where Will Beddows's thugs had spat on it. 'This word's smudged. It says Blyth...something Hall, near Long Lawford. Well, there can't be many halls in a little place like Long Lawford, can there? It shouldn't be hard to find.'

'We don't know Long Lawford. Is it far?' asked Eliza.

'It's near Rugby. In the middle of the country,' Missus Sackman explained. 'My sister lives not far from Rugby. On the way to Birmingham.'

I'd heard people talk about Birmingham and I knew it was quite a way from London. 'Will it take long to walk there?' I asked.

Missus Sackman shook her head as she poured the tea. 'You ain't walking nowhere, my dear.'

The, to our surprise, Mister Sackman smiled as if he was in on some kind of secret. 'How would you like to go on one of them new-fangled trains, eh?' he said.

The three of us looked at each other and grinned. Travel by train? I'd never dreamed of such a thing. Even with all that digging on the rail lines I never thought I'd get to ride on one.

'We'd really like that,' said Eliza. 'That would be grand.'

'Well,' said Mister Sackman, 'my wife and I have agreed that I shall buy you all tickets to Rugby. It's the least I can do after saving my dear Nellie from a dangerous criminal. You'll be with your grandfather in no time at all, I'll see to that.'

Missus Sackman smiled as she handed him a cup of tea. 'That's very kind of you, dear,' she said before turning to us and adding, 'He wants to make up for the trouble he's caused, see. He knew it was wrong.'

The pawnbroker, nodded. 'Indeed I do, wife.' And he took a mouthful of tea. 'We'll have a bite to eat and then we'll set off for Euston station. With a bit of luck, you'll be with your grandfather before bedtime.'

Twenty-Seven
Euston station

Before we left, Missus Sackman made a real fuss about the train journey. 'Them carriages must be cold. You'll need to wrap up warm,' she said. 'I've seen them third-class carriages, they ain't got no roof. What if it rains?'

Mister Sackman patted his wife affectionately on the shoulder. 'Then we'll find 'em some clothes, eh? There's plenty in the shop. A good coat and some strong boots will do the job.'

Missus Sackman was very pleased at his suggestion and she took us into the shop and showed us a box filled with clothes of every kind.

'You look in there, my dears, and sort out something for yourselves,' she said. 'Something good and thick to keep out the cold.'

We didn't need asking twice. We went rummaging in the box, pulling things out and trying them on. They were fine clothes with scarcely a patch on them – just some little holes where the moths had been nibbling and some bigger holes that had been carefully darned. But they had years of wear left in them and they were better than anything we'd had since living in Devil's Acre.

I found Alfie and me jackets made of good wool and hardly worn at all. Mine was brown and Alfie's was grey and they fitted us perfect with plenty of room for growing. Eliza found a grey wool skirt and a big checked shawl with fringing.

'It's ever so warm,' she said. 'I could go out in a snow storm and not get cold.'

When it came to the boots, we thought we were in heaven.

'It's such a long time since I had boots, Missus Sackman,' I said, 'I've forgotten what it's like to wear 'em.' And as I said that, I remembered Mister Dickens and how he'd given us the money for boots. Pity it got stolen.

We all found boots to fit. 'I can wriggle my toes in mine,' said Eliza. 'Real comfy they are and ever so smart looking. I'll be a real lady with these on my feet.'

But when Alfie went to put his on, Missus Sackman saw the cut on his foot and said, 'That needs cleaning up, little man,' and she fetched a bowl of water and a clean cloth for a bandage. 'It don't look good,' she said, shaking her head. 'You'll have to look after this, Alfie. Don't go getting dirt in it.' But once he'd put his boots on, he went stomping round the shop like a soldier on parade. His sore foot didn't seem to bother him at all.

Eliza found a bonnet and I had a new cap but Alfie didn't want one. 'I like the one I've got,' he insisted. So he kept the battered old top hat Uncle Bert had left behind.

By the time we'd put on trousers and shirts, we looked like real toffs – and that's a fact.

Missus Sackman took us into the back room, wiped our hands and faces with a damp flannel then paraded us in front of Mister Sackman. 'Don't they look as smart as paint, husband?'

'Indeed they do, wife,' he said, smiling again and I thought he was a kind old cove, really. He'd made a terrible mistake, thinking we was murderers. But he was only looking after Missus Sackman, see.

I put the letters in the pocket of my new jacket and then it was time to go.

'We'll walk with you to the station and put you on the train,' Mister Sackman said.

'Can you manage the walk up to Euston, dear?' his wife asked. 'I know your bunions are playing you up.'

'What's bunions?' asked Alfie.

'Painful toes what swell a bit like onions,' said Missus Sackman, and Alfie thought this was a fine joke.

'Onions and bunions!' he laughed and Mister Sackman couldn't help laughing, too.

'I'll manage, missus,' he said. 'I want to see these scalliwags on board one o' them trains.' He winked at us. 'You'll like that, won't you?'

We could hardly wait to go. Alfie bounced up and down, singing a silly song about bunions while Missus Sackman looked for a new piece of rope for Patch.

'Do you think Grandpa will like dogs?' Alfie asked.

'A brave dog like your Patch?' said Missus Sackman. 'I should say so!'

151

Then we all stepped into the street, excited to be on our way. The sun came out from behind the clouds as we walked up Whitehall, and when we reached Trafalgar Square, Alfie stopped and pointed to the column in the middle.

'Who's that man on top? What's he doing up there?'

I could tell Mister Sackman was glad of the rest on account of his bunions. 'That's Admiral Nelson, son. He was a fine sailor, he was.' The pawnbroker seemed pleased to tell Alfie what he knew. 'The Admiral was in hundreds of battles and he had his arm chopped off in one of 'em. And his eye was blown out in another.'

Alfie shivered. 'I bet that hurt.'

'It did. But he was real brave, he was.'

'How do you know?'

'My old dad sailed on Nelson's ship when he was a lad.'

'Did he?' said Alfie, very impressed. 'Then why isn't he up on that column?'

'He's not up there cos he wouldn't be able to stand, that's why. His legs was blown off, see. Never sailed again, poor—'

'Mister Sackman!' his wife called. 'That's quite enough of your tales.' But I saw her smile and I don't think she was as cross as she pretended to be.

It was about half an hour before we reached the railway station at Euston, by which time Mister Sackman's bunions were playing up something shocking and he didn't say much. But we pretended not to notice. We were too excited about meeting Grandpa.

'Is that the station?' asked Eliza pointing at a grand

building with a stone roof and several columns.

Missus Sackman squeezed her hand. 'I believe that's called the Euston Arch. It's the entrance, dear. Ain't it grand?'

I didn't like it much. I didn't think a railway station should look like that. 'It looks like a church,' I said, remembering the one in our village.

As we walked into the enormous entrance hall, we all stood gaping up at the ceiling. The hall was huge, it was; as high as a cathedral and there were flights of stairs and eight statues.

'Oh, ain't it fine?' gasped Eliza

'Lawks!' I said, scratching my head. 'I ain't seen nothing like it.'

'Neither have I,' said Missus Sackman, staring wide-eyed, trying to take it all in. 'This must be the Great Hall what they opened last year. But I ain't seen it before. Oh, it's every bit as grand and they said it was.'

Poor Mister Sackman was finding it hard to keep up and when he finally came limping after us, he said, 'Now let's get them tickets, shall we? I expect you want to be on your way.'

The booking office was near the second-class waiting room. We joined the small queue of passengers waiting to buy tickets and we shuffled along behind them until we reached the pay window.

'Three children's tickets for Rugby,' Mister Sackman said to the man behind the glass.

The man leaned forward. 'There's only one third-class train from here and it runs at seven forty-five every morning.'

'Third class?' Mister Sackman replied. 'Who said anything

about third class? I'll have three second class tickets, if you please.' And he turned and winked at us.

The man behind the glass nodded. 'Very well, sir. That will be fifteen shillings and sixpence.'

When Mister Sackman heard that, he turned so pale I thought he was going to faint. It was a whopping price to pay. But he dipped into his pocket like a good un and paid up.

Missus Sackman beamed with pleasure. 'Second class has got a roof on,' she whispered. 'You'll be nice and warm.'

The man behind the glass slid the tickets across to Mister Sackman. 'The train leaves in ten minutes.'

'Where do we find this train?' asked Mister Sackman.

'On the departure stage, sir,' the ticket officer replied with a sigh. 'That's where all the trains leave from.'

We ran to the platform with the sign 'Departure' which was even more exciting that the grand entrance hall. There was a massive roof over the two tracks held up by great cast-iron columns. And best of all – our train was ready and waiting. And what a sight it was! It was huge and the engine was painted black with a brass number thirty-five fixed on the tall chimney which was already puffing out clouds of grey smoke.

Poor Mister Sackman, his bunions were throbbing something terrible and he had a hard time catching up with us, but he managed it in the end.

Eliza pointed to a man standing by the front of the train. 'Who's that?' she asked.

'That's the engine driver,' he told her.

'And why's that man shovelling coal?' asked Alfie.

'He's firing up the engine. It's hot work, that is.'

Eliza shook her head. 'He must be real strong to shovel coal all day.'

Missus Sackman agreed. 'But if he don't do it, the train won't go anywhere, see.'

As we walked down the platform, smoke started puffing towards us and then more noise as a train came into the station along the arrivals track, its huge wheels making a deafening clanking. The smoke was everywhere; puffing out of the chimney, billowing down the platform with its peculiar, musty smell.

Patch was terrified, whimpering and hiding behind Alfie's legs so he picked him up and tucked him inside his jacket.

'We'd best be quick,' said Missus Sackman. 'Your train's going to leave soon.'

We hurried along the platform – except Mister Sackman who could only limp. We passed the first-class carriages where toffs were climbing on board with their wives dressed up in their finery.

When we came to the second-class carriages, Missus Sackman told us to look out for some seats. We saw bank clerks and businessmen pushing and shoving, trying to get seats for themselves so we walked right down to the end of the train where I spotted a space enough for the three of us.

We hugged Missus Sackman and said thank you over and over. And we shook hands with Mister Sackman who smiled and winked at us. Then Alfie climbed into our carriage with Patch and Eliza following behind.

Just as I went to get in, Missus Sackman called me back. 'Sam! Wait! Here, take this.' She pulled something out from under her shawl. 'I thought you should have your box back,' she said. 'It was your ma's, after all.' She gave it to me, smiling and nodding. 'It's only right, my dear.'

And Mister Sackman nodded, too. 'It's only right, lad.'

I was ever so pleased to have it back. 'Thank you both,' I said. 'We won't never forget you.' And I climbed into the carriage.

When the whistle blew, we all leaned out of the window, waving and shouting, 'Goodbye! Goodbye!' while Missus Sackman called, 'Take care, my dears,' and flapped her handkerchief and tried to choke back her tears.

'Write and let us know how…' Mister Sackman called but there was so much noise from the train as it pulled away, it was hard to hear what he said. Then the engine belched out great clouds of smoke and, before we knew it, they had disappeared from view.

Twenty-Eight
High-speed travel

Inside the crowded railway carriage there were two benches –
one on each side. We were squashed together in the
corner by the window. I had Alfie on my knee and Eliza
had Patch.

The men who filled the other seats were an unruly lot,
talking in loud voices and laughing. But they didn't bother us.
They were all working men with mufflers round their necks
and cloth caps on their heads or battered top hats like Uncle
Bert's. It turned out that they were on their way to
Birmingham to find work.

As the train drew away from the station, I checked
my pocket to make sure that the tickets were still there.
We had to get off at Rugby and then we'd ask the way to Long
Lawford. Missus Sackman hadn't thought it would be much
of a walk.

'I've got a surprise,' I whispered to the others.

'What?' asked Alfie.

Then I pulled out the silver box.

'Oh, Sam!' said Eliza. 'Ma's box! We got it back. Everything's going to be all right – I know it.'

'We can show it to Grandpa,' said Alfie bouncing up and down on my knee. 'We'll soon be there, won't we?' But I couldn't help wondering, what if he didn't want us?

Once the train picked up speed, it began to shake. And that was when Eliza got upset.

'Oh lawks!' she cried, hugging Patch to her chest. 'It's going too fast. My head going to blow off if it don't stop soon.' She grabbed hold of my arm. 'It ain't natural, is it? I've never known anything travel this fast. It's dangerous, this is.'

'I like it,' Alfie grinned while I tried to calm my sister.

'It ain't that bad, Eliza,' I said. 'I heard the queen travelled in a train just the other day. She didn't die, did she?'

'No, but I bet she hated it! And so do I.'

I squeezed her hand and pretended to be brave, but truth was I was feeling nervous myself. Was it any wonder? I'd only ever travelled by horse and cart – and that was fast enough for me. Why would anybody need to go faster? I shut my eyes and tried to think of our old home in the country with Ma and Pa. I thought about sheep and cows. I thought about picking apples and blackberries. But it didn't help. The men's chatter and the thick smoke from their pipes, made my head spin something shocking. Then there was the rocking and shaking of the train making my stomach churn so bad, it gave me the collywobbles.

The noise of the wheels seemed to say, 'Head, stomach. Head, stomach.' And I couldn't help groaning. I tried to stop the terrible feeling in my belly. I was the oldest. The man of the family. I couldn't throw up. I couldn't.

But suddenly I leaped to my feet, pushing Alfie off my lap. I lurched forward, stuck my head out of the window and was violently sick.

When I returned to my seat my cheeks were red with embarrassment. The men guffawed and slapped me on the back while I wiped the sick from my mouth with the end of my sleeve.

'You kids ain't up to this travelling lark,' laughed one. 'You'll get used to it, lad.'

I didn't want to get used to it. The journey seemed much too long and the day was getting colder. We huddled together for warmth and eventually I fell asleep to the rocking motion of the train. Even the men went quiet and when, sometime later, I opened my eyes, there was only the sound of the wheels on the track – *chiggerty chig…chiggerty chig…chiggerty chig…* Daylight was fading.

Alfie dug his elbow into my side. 'Sam,' he whispered in my ear.

'What is it?' I groaned

'I need a wee.'

'Don't think about it,' I said. 'Just wait until we get to Rugby. It can't be long now. Go back to sleep.'

'I can't,' said Alfie, wriggling on my knee. 'I'm bursting.'

I tried to distract him with looking for things out of the window, but it was lucky that five minutes later, the train slowed down and pulled up. We heard the station master calling, 'Rugby station! Alight here for Rugby.'

Glad that the journey was over, we flung the door open and jumped down onto the platform.

'I'm going for a wee,' said Alfie dashing straight for the embankment, which was thick with trees and bushes. We stood on the platform where the station master in his long coat and top hat was waiting to blow his whistle for the train to leave.

'Can you help us, mister?' I asked when the train had gone. 'We've got to go to this place,' I said, showing him the letter with the address on it.

He took the letter and held it close. 'It's a bit smudged,' he said, squeezing his eyes. 'I can just make out the letter "B" and I can see "Hall".' He looked down at us and smiled. 'I'm almost certain you'll be wanting Blythwell Hall.'

'It ain't far, is it?' asked Eliza. 'I'm worn out with all this travelling. It ain't natural if you ask me.'

The station master smiled. 'No, it's not far, missy.'

When Alfie came back with Patch the station master took us to the entrance and pointed down a narrow road. 'Go that way for half a mile till you come to a signpost. Go straight past it and you'll come to the Hall. You'll be there in no time. Half an hour or so. They're expecting you, are they?'

'Our grandpa's rich,' said Alfie, as usual. 'We're going to be looked after and have a nice comfy bed and blankets and everything.'

The station master patted him on the shoulder. 'Course you are, lad,' he said. 'Now wrap your muffler around your neck. It's cold tonight. Take care now.' And we set off down a narrow country road, hoping we would reach Grandpa's house before it went dark.

Twenty-Nine

Blythwell Hall

We never saw anything on that road — not a man or a cart. We didn't meet a soul all the time we were walking. That road seemed to go on and on, like it never went anywhere. We were all tired and, to make matters worse, it was hard to see our way.

As time passed, it grew dark and a bitter wind sprang up. Alfie and me pulled our mufflers tight round our necks and buttoned our jackets, trying to stay warm, while Eliza wrapped her shawl around her chest. Then, worst luck, it started to rain — heavy, driving rain that soaked through our clothes in no time at all. Eliza and Alfie looked as miserable as I felt. Who wouldn't be miserable with wet clothes and an empty belly?

But we trudged on passed the signpost, heads down against the rain, hoping that every step was taking us closer to Grandpa.

'Are we definitely going the right way?' Eliza asked eventually.

'The man at the station said just keep going.'

'Well, I hopes you're right, Sam Pargeter,' she snapped. 'What if we should have turned up that lane back there? We'll be wandering along this road all night. Die of cold, we will.'

I didn't admit she could be right. I just crossed my fingers and tried not to panic.

After what felt like hours, the rain eased off. Clouds blew away and the moon came out again so it was easier to see where we were going.

'Are we nearly there?' Alfie kept asking until I got annoyed and told him to stow it. Then he went all grizzly and sat on the wet grass.

'My foot hurts,' he said, rubbing his eyes. 'Even with my new boots, my foot hurts, it does.' And he began to cry.

What could I do? I lifted him up and he hung over my shoulder like one of them rag dolls and fell asleep.

Alfie was heavy and I was tired so I had to slow down. The road ahead seemed like it went on and on. No wider than a farm track. I was thinking Eliza was right when she said we'd be wandering along all night. But suddenly the road turned to the right and when we walked round the bend, we saw something in the distance.

'What's that?' said Eliza.

I squinted but clouds passed over the moon and it went dark so I couldn't see.

'Wait till we're closer,' I said. 'It might be nothing.' We plodded on. *Please let it be Grandpa's house*, I whispered under my breath. *Please, please, please!*

Another thirty yards and Eliza suddenly squealed, 'Gates, Sam! I can see some gates!' and she raced towards them.

Eliza's shout woke Alfie and he slipped from my shoulder. Forgetting about his sore foot, he raced over to her but I didn't have the energy to run.

'I'm coming, Eliza,' I called and tried to make my legs move faster.

When I finally got there, I saw a pair of gates, tall as a house. Long ago, they must have been grand but now they were old and rusty.

'Look, Sam,' Eliza said pointing to the wall by the side of the gates. 'I can see something.'

I went over to look and there, carved into the wall, were the words *Blythwell Hall*. At last we had reached Grandpa's house!

Eliza began leaping and dancing around as if she had just got out of bed. She tried lifting the handle on the gate but it was stiff and, being a girl, she couldn't manage it, see.

'You girls ain't strong enough,' I joked, my bad mood gone now that we were here.

'Oh no?' said Eliza. 'But girls ain't half clever.'

I grinned and turned the handle as easy as you like and pushed the gates open.

We ran down the long drive, overgrown with shrubs and bushes, until we came to a big patch of grass with a huge cedar tree set in the middle. Its branches were so long and heavy that they drooped down and touched the grass. The tree looked terrifying in the moonlight and for a minute, we stood open mouthed. But I took a deep breath and looked beyond it, and there it was – a rambling old house

'That's it,' I said. 'We've found it!'

'Grandpa's house,' shouted Alfie. 'Oh, ain't it grand?'

We couldn't stop him. He raced ahead towards the front

door with Patch keeping up on his three good legs. We hurried after him, but when we got near to the house, I could see that Blythwell Hall wasn't as grand as I thought. The window frames were rotting in parts. So I wondered if maybe the old man didn't care about such things. Some people don't, do they? Not everybody likes new painted windows.

We stood at the front door and stared at its peeling black paint. I didn't say anything to the others – but it crossed my mind that Grandpa might be poor now and living in a tumble-down wreck. So what if he was poor? He was our Grandpa, wasn't he? And we would have a roof over our heads and maybe some food. That wasn't so bad. Better than Devil's Acre. Better than the workhouse.

'Who's going to tug the bell pull?' I asked, grinning at Alfie, trying to hide my nervousness.

'Me! Me!' he insisted, jumping up and down, trying to reach it. 'Give me a leg up, Sam.'

I tucked him under my arm and lifted him so he could pull on the chain. A solemn clanging echoed down the hall like a funeral bell and soon died away. We waited for a while then Alfie made a fuss and wanted to try again. Before the second clanging had stopped, we heard slow, shuffling footsteps coming towards the door. Eliza clutched onto my jacket and Alfie onto my leg as bolts were drawn back and a key was turned in the lock.

There was a great deal of creaking hinges as the door opened – but only wide enough to see a face and a flickering candle. The face was grey and thin with eyes set deep and a

164

nose that sprouted like a parrot's beak between them. It was the face of a very old man.

'Who are you?' he demanded.

'We've come to see Sir Samuel Pargeter,' I said, my heart pounding in my chest.

He opened the door a little wider, squeezing his eyes and staring at me. 'Speak up, boy. Don't mumble.'

'We've come to see Sir Samuel Pargeter,' I repeated, trying to make my voice heard above the wind.

'Still can't hear yer,' grumbled the old cove. 'You'd better come in and see the master. He'll sort you out.' He turned and shuffled away down the gloomy hall, his back bent, carrying the candle.

Alfie put the rope round Patch's neck and we followed. At the end of the hall, the old man turned down a passageway, as gloomy as the first, and he stopped outside a door and knocked.

'Enter!' boomed a deep voice and he opened it and stepped inside.

'Children,' the old man announced. I thought it was odd, him saying just one word like that.

Then the deep voice said, 'Children? Did you say "children", Smidgeby?'

'Aye,' said the old man. 'Children. They come to the front door.'

'Where have they come from? Who sent them?'

'How do I know? They talk in whispers.'

'Then send them in, Smidgeby.'

The old man came back into the passage. But he didn't speak to us. He just shoved us into the room one by one. He tried to take hold of Patch's rope but when the dog growled and bared his teeth, Smidgeby changed his mind and let him go with Alfie.

I tell you, my heart was a-bumping and a-pounding fit to burst as we stepped into that room. But it was grand and as warm as crumpets. Grandpa was sitting in an armchair by the fire. He was quite old – though not very old – with a round red face and thinning hair. His clothes were fine enough but his red waistcoat was tight over his stomach. I thought this was a good sign, showing that he must have eaten a great deal of the best food. There was a roaring fire in the grate and there were five oil lamps around the room so you could see every corner. I needn't have worried. Grandpa was wealthy for sure.

When he turned and looked up at us, he smiled and said, 'Well, well, well. You look like three promising young things. Have you come far?'

'We have,' said Alfie who couldn't wait to answer. 'We come from London, we did. And we come on a train. But it took a long time and it was cold and we had to walk...'

'Indeed,' said Grandpa. 'And who sent you to me, may I ask?'

'Our Aunt Maud and Uncle Bert,' I said, stepping nearer. 'They told us to come and find you. I'm Sam, and this is Eliza and Alfie.'

'I see. Do I know your aunt and uncle? What is their surname?'

'Bagstone,' I said. 'Aunt Maud was our ma's sister.'

Eliza jumped in then, eager to tell a part of the story. 'Ma died, see. And our father was in foreign parts so we didn't have nowhere to go except to Aunt Maud. But Uncle Bert gambled all his money away and we finished up in Devil's Acre and—'

He held up his hand for her to stop. 'I'm afraid I don't know any Bagstones,' he said, shaking his head. 'I've met a good many people in London but never a Bagstone.'

I pulled out the silver box and put it on a small round table. Then I took out the letter Aunt Maud had written. 'She sent you this,' I said and handed it to him.

He raised his eyebrows as he slowly unfolded the piece of paper and read what she had written.

Dear Sir Samuel Pargeter,

I am in terrible trouble of the money kind and cannot look after your grandchildren any longer. I know you are a wealthy man. For the sake of your son's memory, please take care of them.

Your humble servant,

Maud Bagstone.

'Well,' he said handing back the letter. 'Now I understand.' He pulled out his handkerchief and wiped his forehead which was sweating from the heat of the fire. He pushed himself up out of his chair and stood up in front of us, his hands folded across his stomach. And then came the worst news.

'I'm afraid you have made a mistake,' he said. 'You see, I am not Sir Samuel Pargeter and I am not your grandfather.'

Thirty
Meeting the Mogwurts

I was confused. If the master of the house wasn't our grandpa, we must have come to the wrong place. How could that be? I'd followed the directions.

'But the man at the station told us how to get here, didn't he, Sam?' Eliza protested.

'He did,' I said. 'He pointed down the road and said go straight on and you'll get there.'

By then Eliza was in a right temper. 'He shouldn't have said that, mister. We walked and walked to get here. We thought we was—'

The gentleman coughed to interrupt her. 'He made a mistake, my dear,' he said. 'He sent you to Blythwell Hall. I expect he thought you were new pupils.'

'Pupils?' I said. 'Is this a school or somethink? It don't look like any school I've seen.'

'It is the finest!' the gentleman declared, tucking his thumbs into the pockets of his waistcoat. 'My name is Ebenezer Mogwurt and I am proud to be the proprietor of this splendid school. Many people send their youngsters here to receive a superb education. The best in the land.'

'That may be so,' I said. 'But we're not looking for a heducation. We're looking for our grandpa.'

Alfie was puzzled by all this talk about schooling. He tugged the man's sleeve and said, 'If our grandpa ain't here, where is he? What you done with him, mister?'

Mister Mogwurt coughed again. 'I'll explain,' he said, clasping his hands together and leaning forward as if he were about to tell us a bedtime story. 'I think I can help you for I have met Sir Samuel...er...several times. He is a fine gentleman. Why, I spoke to him only last Christmas. He lives two miles or so from here in a grand house called Blythfield Hall which stands at the top of a hill.'

'Blyth*field?*' I said.

'Yes. You see, how similar the name is. This is Blythwell Hall.' He laughed. 'They are easily confused.'

'Right then. Sorry to have bothered you, mister. We'd best be off.'

'Perhaps you could tell us how to get to Blythfield Hall, mister?' asked Eliza. 'We're that tired we could sleep standing up, we could. But we want to be off and out of your way.'

Mister Mogwurt rubbed his chin. 'I'm sure I can be of help,' he said glancing at the silver box. 'I've taken to you, and I'd be prepared to lend you the services of my manservant in exchange for...er...that small box.'

He reached out to take it, but I got there before him.

'That's Ma's,' I said, shocked.

He shrugged. 'It isn't worth much but it's a small price to

170

pay, is it not? My man will fetch a lantern and take you to your grandfather at once.'

I was about to say, 'No thank you very much,' when the door opened and a woman came hurrying into the room. She was tall and thin and dressed in purple. On her head was a peculiar knot of black hair. When she saw us, she stopped and stared, not looking at all pleased to see three wet and muddy children with a dog in her parlour.

'Explain yourself, Mister Mogwurt,' she demanded, her face as sharp and frosty as a winter's morning. 'Why are these filthy urchins standing on my best carpet? New pupils don't belong in here, as you very well know.'

Mister Mogwurt cheeks flushed scarlet. 'These are not pupils, my dear,' he said, holding up his hands. 'No, no, no. They are lost and on their way to find their grandfather, Sir Samuel Pargeter and—'

Before Mister Mogwurt could say more, the woman interrupted him. 'Did you say Sir Samuel Pargeter?' she asked.

'Er, yes, dear.'

'And he is their grandfather?'

Mister Mogwurt nodded.

'Are you sure, husband?'

He nodded again.

Then Missus Mogwurt turned to us, suddenly smiling in a most peculiar way. 'So Sir Samuel is your grandfather. And is he expecting you tonight?'

Alfie grinned and stepped forward. 'No, missus. It's going to be a big surprise, see. He ain't never seen us before.'

At these words, Missus Mogwurt's face lit up – like a nipper on Christmas Day who's found the best present ever – and I wondered why. She clapped her hands. 'Oh, but you cannot walk all the way to Blythfield Hall in the dark. It must be five miles or more. Who knows what villains are out there? No! You must stay the night.'

'But, my dear…' protested Mister Mogwurt. 'They are anxious to see their grandfather.'

All of a sudden, his wife's happy expression disappeared from her face like butter in a frying pan. She gritted her teeth and said, 'That is not a good idea, husband.' Then she turned back to us with a smile. 'You are wet and hungry, my dears. I insist you have a meal of my delicious homemade pie and a comfortable bed. Tomorrow will be early enough for you to see your grandfather.'

Alfie, stamped his foot, 'No, it won't. I want to go now!'

Missus Mugwort placed her hand on Alfie's shoulder and gripped him tightly. 'You wouldn't want to give the dear old man a fright, would you, eh?' She gripped tighter so that her fingers dug deep. 'Finding you on his doorstep after dark – why, he might be scared out of his wits.'

There was something about Missus Mogwurt that wasn't right. She was all smiles on the outside but on the inside I thought she might have a nasty streak. What she was saying was sensible, though. We were soaked to the skin and freezing cold – so I nodded.

She released her grip on Alfie and headed for the door. 'Smidgeby!' she shouted several times until the old man appeared.

172

'Take these young persons to the dining room, if you please. They are hungry and need feeding.'

Smidgeby's eyebrows shot up as if he had never heard such a thing before. He gawped at her and said, 'The *dining room?*'

I wondered if he hadn't heard her properly on account of him being a bit deaf. I noticed Missus Mogwurt pressing her lips together trying to keep her temper.

'The dining room,' she repeated through gritted teeth. 'They shall have the rabbit pie, Smidgeby. With treacle tart and custard to follow.'

'Rabbit pie and treacle tart?' Smidgeby gasped.

Then Mister Mogwurt looked alarmed. 'But, my dear, I was looking forward to your rabbit pie. You know it—'

His wife glowered at him again and he snapped his mouth shut, obviously not daring to say more.

She turned to us, smiling again. 'I have a most delicious pie and treacle tart,' she said. 'Would you like that?' We all nodded. Of course we would. We were starving and our mouths were already watering at the very thought of it.

'They're kind folks, ain't they, Alfie?' Eliza whispered as we followed Smidgeby into the dining room. 'We'll have a feast and a comfy bed tonight and we'll see Grandpa tomorrow. Ain't we the lucky ones?'

But I wasn't so sure.

Thirty-One

A night at Blythwell Hall

Smidgeby took us into the dining room where a square table was set with a white linen cloth and silver knives and forks. Logs were burning in a big fireplace and made the room so cosy that our toes tingled and our wet clothes began to steam as they dried.

We sat waiting while Smidgeby disappeared to fetch the food.

'You got the box, Sam?' asked Eliza. 'You ain't lost nothing, have yer?'

'Inside my jacket,' I said. 'I put the letters in it. It's safe.'

When Smidgeby returned, he served up a stupendous rabbit pie with thick brown gravy and a pile of boiled potatoes.

While we were eating we could hear a right barny going on in the parlour next to the dining room. Missus Mugwort was yelling at her husband something shocking. Just another quarrel between a married couple, I thought. Just like Aunt Maud and Uncle Bert.

But the food was so good none of us cared about the shouting. None of us said a word being too busy eatin', see. Alfie didn't forget Patch, though. He dropped pieces of pastry under the table making the little fella very happy indeed.

We thought we couldn't eat another thing, but when Smidgeby brought in treacle tart we somehow managed to scoff that too, smothered with smooth yellow custard.

'That was the best meal ever,' said Eliza, leaning back in her chair and letting out a deep sigh.

'Missus Mogwurt's very kind,' said Alfie. 'That meal was very, very nice.'

'Galopshus, weren't it?' I said. 'If pupils get food like that every day, they must be well pleased.' Suddenly the idea of going to school didn't seem as bad as I'd thought.

Smidgeby grunted in reply as he shuffled round the table clearing away the empty plates. That was when Missus Mogwurt walked in.

'Wonderful!' she said, clapping her hands. 'I see you've eaten everything.'

'Thank you, Missus Mogwurt. I'm full to burstin',' I said and unbuttoned my jacket to give my belly more room. And as I did, the silver box fell on the floor.

Missus Mogwurt looked at it. 'What's this?' she said and picked it up. Her eyes lit up, all excited like.

'It's Ma's box,' Eliza explained. 'The one what Pa gave her.'

'It's real silver,' said Alfie. 'We're taking it to Grandpa's.'

Missus Mogwurt turned the box over in her hands. 'I shall keep it safe for you until tomorrow.'

I had a nasty feeling about this woman. I didn't trust her – nice food or not. 'No need, Missus Mogwurt,' I said. 'I can look after it.'

But she clutched the box tight. 'I insist. I shall put it in a safe place for you. And now it's time you were in bed. You've had a long day.'

I didn't know what else I could do, except make sure we left Blythwell Hall with the box as soon as we could in the morning.

Missus Mogwurt took hold of Alfie's hand and helped him off his chair. 'Now then, young man, let me take you to your bedroom. You'll have a comfortable bed, you'll see. Come. I'll show you.'

She tucked the box into her shawl then picked up an oil lamp in one hand and held Alfie in the other. We followed behind feeling well fed and looking forward to a good night's sleep in a nice bedroom.

As we walked down the corridor, I noticed how cold it was, nothing like the other rooms. I was so cold that I started to shiver and I fastened my jacket and pulled my muffler round tight round my neck.

This part of the house was odd. There had once been wallpaper on the walls but now it was hanging off and, in places, water was trickling down from the ceiling. There was the terrible smell too. I couldn't tell what it was but it grew stronger as we walked along the passage. It made my stomach churn, I tell you. It was something like over-cooked cabbage mixed with a slop bucket.

Alfie clapped his hand over his mouth. 'It stinks down here,' he wailed. 'I feel sick.'

Missus Mogwurt stroked his head. 'Oh, no. You've

probably eaten too much. Sometimes it's hard for boys not to be so greedy.'

But there were noises too. Further along the miserable passage, we heard shouting and sobbing like children in pain. Was I imagining things? Maybe I was too tired and in need of a good sleep. But I couldn't shake off the feeling that I'd done the wrong thing in agreeing to spend the night here. What was this place?

Missus Mugwort stopped by a door and let go of Alfie's hand. She pulled out a bunch of keys hanging from a chain around her waist. 'This is the guest room,' she said, like she was a toff in a big house. She turned a large iron key in the lock and threw open the door.

We were in for a nasty surprise. The room wasn't much better than the one in Devil's Acre —cold, with bare walls and just a small window at the far end. There were four metal beds – two on one side and two on the other – with a thin mattress and a blanket on each. The only other thing, apart from the chamber pot, was a small table with half a candle set in an old candle stick.

After the smart parlour and dining room, we were disappointed, I can tell you. Our faces must have shown that we'd expected better. But Missus Mogwurt didn't seem to notice.

'Now, my dears,' she said. 'I see that your poor clothes are wet and muddy.'

'They ain't so wet now,' Alfie replied.

But Missus Mogwurt held out her hand. 'Give them to me

and I'll see that they are dried properly and brushed clean before morning.'

Alfie made a fuss. 'No, I don't want to,' he said. 'They're mine.'

'Come on, Alfie,' Eliza said. 'The kind lady's going to dry 'em. You'll have 'em back tomorrow.'

Alfie and me took off the jackets Missus Sackman had given us, and our trousers and even our mufflers. Eliza removed her grey skirt and checked shawl and handed them over.

'Boots, too,' insisted Missus Mogwurt.

'Don't want to,' said Alfie, hugging them to his chest. He'd never had such a good pair of boots, see. Though I admit they were covered in mud.

'Now, now,' said Missus Mogwurt. 'You want to look smart for your grandfather, don't you? I'll make sure they're cleaned and polished ready for you to wear tomorrow.'

By the time she walked out of the room, we were left wearing nothing but thin shirts and petticoats.

'Sleep well,' she called as she turned the key in the lock and left us in that freezing cold room.

We all felt miserable, but I tried not to show it for the sake of the others. 'This is better than sleeping in a ditch, ain't it?' I said, trying to cheer 'em up. 'We've got a roof over our heads and we've got a blanket. Not bad, is it?'

'I can't stop shaking, it's that cold,' said Eliza.

'Me, too,' said Alfie. 'Why couldn't we stay by that nice fire?'

'You climb in with him,' I said to Eliza. 'You'll be warmer that way.'

Eliza had never had a bed to herself, so she didn't mind squashing up with Alfie. 'Toasty, ain't it?' she said as she wrapped her arms round him. I put two blankets over them and Patch curled up under the bed.

'Why did she lock the door, Sam?' Eliza asked as she blew out the candle. 'Was she thinking we'd run away or something?'

'Dunno,' I grunted. It was a very good question and I wished I knew the answer. There was something wrong, I could feel it like an itch at the back of my neck. I lay there in the dark, wondering what would happen in the morning and how we would get away from Blythwell Hall.

Thirty-Two

An unexpected visitor

In the middle of the night something woke me. It was Patch and he was growling.

'What's up, boy?' I groaned. 'Go back to sleep.' But he kept on, louder and louder, so I got up and lit the candle.

I held it high so I could see better and there he was at the foot of the bed, his legs quivering and his little ears erect, staring at the door.

'What's he growling for?' asked Eliza as she sat up rubbing her eyes. 'Stop it, Patch.' And she climbed out of bed and went to pick him up.

'He's heard something!' I whispered. 'There's a noise. I can hear it now.'

'What?'

'I don't know. A weird sound. Out in the corridor.'

She hugged Patch tight to stop him growling and sat on the edge of the bed. 'I can hear it,' she said. 'A sort of scratching at the door. Is somebody trying to get in?'

'Maybe.'

It went on for a minute or so. *Scratch, rattle, scratch*. Then it stopped.

'It's gone. Probably a rat or something. Let's get back to sleep.'

Eliza was all of a tremble. 'Was it a ghost, do you think?'

'There ain't no such thing, sis. I'm always telling you that.' I put the candle on the little table and climbed into bed.

But the noise started again – *scratch, rattle, scratch* – louder this time. And it wasn't a rat. I could tell. Somebody was out there trying to get in. We both sat up. Eliza clung onto Patch and pulled the blanket up to her nose. We were both scared out of our skins. Only Alfie slept on.

When the noise stopped, all I could hear was my heart thumping. Then came another sound – different, more scary than the last. It was terrifying. I knew what this one was. It was the creaking and grinding of rusty hinges as the bedroom door slowly swung open.

That was when Alfie woke up and pointed at the door. 'He's comin' to get me! The bad man's takin' me away.'

'Who's there?' I called. 'What's going on?'

My hand was shaking something awful, but I managed to reach for the candlestick and I held it up like a weapon.

A voice came out of the shadows. 'Stow it, will yer? Smidgeby's in the next room. If he hears yer he'll come in and I'll be for it.'

The flame of the candle flickered as a boy, skinny as a whippet, stepped into the room and shut the door behind him. He was barefoot and dressed in a tattered shirt that I guessed had once been white but, for want of a good wash, was now a horrible shade of grey.

'Are you a ghost?' Eliza trembled, holding onto Alfie and Patch. 'You ain't come to haunt us, have yer?'

The boy swaggered towards the beds, twirling a thick piece of wire round his finger. He had probably used it to pick the lock.

'I ain't no ghost.' He grinned. 'I've come visiting, I have. You're the new kids, ain't yer?'

'Who are you?' I asked.

'I'm Dembow,' said the boy. 'Old Smidgeby told us you was here. Three new pupils, he said. So why did the old dragon put you in here instead of with us, eh? What's her game?'

'That's rude, that is,' Eliza replied. 'You shouldn't call Missus Mogwurt a dragon. She was kind, she was. She gave us rabbit pie.'

'Rabbit pie?' Dembow gasped. 'I never heard the like. You rich or somethink?'

'No. And we ain't pupils neither,' I said. 'We're just here for the night, see. We're going to Blythfield Hall in the morning. That's where our grandpa lives.'

'He's a toff, is he?' Dembow asked.

'He's rich!' said Alfie, wriggling out of Eliza's grasp. 'He don't know we're coming so it'll be a nice surprise. And he's going to look after us.'

Dembow sat down on the end the bed and looked at me. 'You sure this rich geezer will take you in?'

I still had the niggling worry at the back of my mind that he might turn us away but I said, 'Course he'll take us in. Why wouldn't he?'

Dembow scratched his head. 'Well, I'm thinkin' that the Mogwurts might be up to their old tricks, see.'

'What are you on about?' I said.

'The old dragon locked you in, didn't she?'

'Yes.'

'Took your clothes, an' all?'

'Yes, so what?'

'Think about it,' said Dembow. 'Why would she do that, eh?'

'Cos, she's kind,' said Alfie, 'and she gives us very nice food. Very, very nice food.'

'Listen,' said Dembow. 'I was down at the other end of the house earlier. Helpin' myself to somethin' to eat – which is one of my specialities, see. And I heard the Mogwurts havin' a real barny.'

'We heard a bit of that, too,' I said. 'But we couldn't hear what they was arguing about.'

'Well, I'll tell yer,' said Dembow. 'Missus Mogwurt's the brains, see. As cunning as a rattle-snake, she is. Always keeps her eye on the money.'

'And did you hear what she said?' I asked.

'I did,' he said, leaning forward and tapping the side of his nose. 'She's got a plan.'

'What kind of plan?'

'Tomorrow mornin', she's sendin' her husband up to see Sir Samuel Pargeter.'

'That's our grandpa, that is,' said Eliza. 'Are we going with him?'

Dembow shook his head. 'No, you can't cos he's goin' to

tell the old man that his long-lost grandchildren have turned up at the Blythwell Hall by mistake and they're wantin' to come to live with him.'

'We'll see our grandpa!' said Alfie as chirpy as you like. 'Hurray!'

'That's good, ain't it?' asked Eliza.

'No. Not good,' said Dembow. 'He'll tell your grandpa what horrible little rogues you are, covered in fleas and with shockin' bad manners. Not the kind of children he'd want in his fine house.'

'But why would Mister Mugwort say things like that?' asked Eliza. 'What's the point?'

I thought I understood. 'Mister Mugwort will offer to keep us on as pupils in his school here. I expect he'll promise to look after us and give us a fine education, eh?'

Dembow nodded. 'You got it exactly right. Sir Samuel's very rich, so they say, and they'll make him pay a high price – for years and years.' He sighed. 'That's what they always do... I know cos there's fourteen of us kids here, see, and it happened to all of us. None of our families wanted us so they sent us here and paid the Mogwurts to keep us.'

'That's horrible,' said Eliza. 'No! That can't be right.'

Dembow stood up. 'Come and see if you don't believe me,' he said beckoning us to follow. 'Bring yer candle and keep quiet.'

We left the room, wondering where we were being taken. Alfie held Patch so he wouldn't make a noise and I carried the candle, which cast black shadows on the walls of the narrow corridor. The stone floor was freezing to our feet. At the end, we turned down a passage and stopped outside a door.

'This is it,' he said.

'This is what?' I asked as he opened the door.

'Take a look for yourselves.'

I leaned forward into the room, holding the candle high so we could see. Lying on the stone floor were a dozen or more children, dressed in tattered shirts with only a thin blanket for cover. One or two raised their heads, their eyes sunken with dark circles. One sat up and called out, 'Is that you, Mister Smidgeby? Is it time to get up?'

Dembow said, 'Go to sleep, little uns,' and he pulled the miserable thin blanket over them as they lay down again. All except for two boys over in the corner. One was sobbing something shocking while the other had his arms round him like a mother.

'What's up, Jimmie?' asked Dembow, stepping over the other kids to reach him.

It was the other little un what spoke.

'He's had one of his dreams,' he said. 'He thought he was up that chimney again.'

At the word 'chimney' Jimmie started to scream but Dembow grabbed hold of him and pulled him to his chest to deaden the noise. 'Shhhh, Jimmie,' he said, stroking his hair. 'You're not stuck up that chimney no more. You're here with your mates. Safe and sound.' Dembow was obviously something of a leader here and the little boy stared at him, his eyes wide and trusting. 'Anyway,' said Dembow, 'you're growing that fast you'll soon be too big to go sweepin'.' He grinned. 'Look. I got something special for yer.' And he pulled a piece of beef out of his shirt pocket and popped it into Jimmy's mouth.

'Where's their beds?' asked Alfie, but Eliza tugged his hand and pulled him away.

'Sam, let's get out of here!' she said.

'Seen enough, have yer?' Dembow asked.

I was too shocked to speak. We just nodded and followed our new friend back down the corridor. I couldn't help thinking about the boys in *Oliver Twist*. Fagin's boys. But that was a story. This was real and all the worse for it.

Back in the room where we were sleeping, Dembow perched on the edge of the bed.

'How long you been in this place?' I asked.

'Two years,' he replied. 'Pa died and Ma married again, see. Her new husband didn't want me gettin' in the way so he sent me here.' He chewed on his fingernail. 'Everybody's got the same story. Nobody wants us. That's why our stepfathers or grandfathers or uncles and aunts pay the Mogwurts to keep us, see.'

'But this is a school, ain't it?' I asked.

'Call it a school?' Dembow sneered. 'Funny sort of school wot gives lessons in cleaning chimneys and digging in the fields from sunrise till after dark. Funny school wot feeds yer gruel as thin as water.'

Eliza screwed up her face. 'That can't be right,' she said. 'Missus Mogwurt's food is scrummy. We had treacle tart

186

and—'

'Scrummy?' said Dembow. 'A bowl of gruel a day – that's what we get. Do you call that scrummy? If I wasn't so fly at picking locks an' stealin' bits o' grub, we'd be walkin' skeletons, I tell yer!'

At last I was realising the truth of it. We weren't no more than prisoners.

'We've got to get out of here,' I said.

'But they've taken our clothes,' said Eliza. 'We've no boots. No nothing!'

I remembered something else and groaned. 'And they've got the box with the letters. Even if we get to Blythfield Hall, we've got nothing to show Grandpa. Nothing to prove that we're his grandchildren.'

A tear trickled down Eliza's cheek and she covered her face with her hands. 'That's it! This time we're done for, ain't we?'

Thirty-Three

Dembow's plan

Things looked grim, but Dembow was a cheery soul and wasn't downhearted.

'Never give up, girl,' he said, jumping off the bed and slapping Eliza on the shoulder. 'I might be able to help yer.'

'You?' she snorted. 'You can't even help yourself. You've been stuck in here for two years. You said so.'

Dembow stood there grinning. 'You've got the advantage of my inside knowledge, ain't yer?' He leaned forward, tapping his nose. 'I'll help you and maybe you can help us, eh?'

There was something I liked about Dembow. Anybody who lived such a miserable life and stayed chirpy as a cricket had to be a good sort.

'So, how can you help us?' I asked.

'Listen,' he said, settling himself back on the bed. 'I'll get them clothes back for yer. The old dragon will have put 'em in a cupboard waitin' till she goes go to Rugby to sell 'em. If there's a lock to pick, I can do it. Easy!'

'She's got our silver box as well,' Eliza explained. 'It was Ma's, and our letters are in it.'

'No problem,' said Dembow. 'I know where it'll be.'

'I'm coming with you,' I said. 'Once we've got our clothes and the box, we'll run away.'

'Yeah!' Alfie shouted, bouncing on the bed. 'Run away! Go to Grandpa's house.'

'Shhhh!' said Eliza and made him sit down.

I suddenly wondered why Dembow hadn't run away himself. So I asked him. 'Why don't you come with us?'

'Can't leave nobody behind. There's too many of us, see. And anyway, we've nowhere to run to except the workhouse.'

It didn't feel right doing a runner and leaving the boys at Blythwell Hall. 'We'll tell our Grandpa what the Mogwurts are up to. He must have rich friends like a magistrate or somebody what could help.'

Eliza liked that. 'They'll arrest 'em for child cruelty, they will. That would be good. Stick 'em in prison, eh?'

We talked about what would happen if we got found out. And what would happen if we managed to escape. We made plans and decided that, first of all, Dembow and me would go looking for the clothes.

'There's a cupboard in the parlour,' said Dembow.

'I've seen it,' I replied.

'We'll try that first. We might be in luck.'

I followed him down the passageway and when we reached the parlour, he looked over his shoulder and pressed a finger to his lips. He put his ear to the door and, when he was satisfied no one was there, he turned slowly opened it. As soon as we stepped into the room, we felt the heat from the fire, still glowing in the grate. Dembow grinned and sat down

189

in one of the armchairs by the hearth. I couldn't resist, and for a minute or so we stretched out our hands and feet to warm them.

When we were nicely toasted, Dembow stood up and nodded towards the far wall where a mahogany cupboard stood beneath portrait of Missus Mogwurt in a red satin dress with a mop of lace set on top of her unnatural black hair. We tiptoed round the chairs towards the cupboard and Dembow kneeled down and pulled the piece of wire from his pocket before pushing it into the keyhole. I lowered the candle so that he could see better and soon he had the door open.

There were three shelves inside, but I couldn't see any clothes. There were drinking glasses and bottles on the top shelf, three square boxes on the next and a warm blanket on the lowest one. The blanket was probably for Missus Mogwurt so she didn't burn her knees when she sat too near the fire. *What about them poor mites sleeping in the cold?* I thought. Couldn't she have given them her blanket?

Before Dembow shut the doors, he reached inside, took one of the boxes from the middle shelf and lifted the lid. Chocolates! Real chocolates like you've never seen. Some square, some round with swirls on the top or little silver balls. They looked amazing. Dembow took one and passed the box to me. I took a round one and bit into it. It was like strawberries and cream and chocolate, all mixed together. I closed my eyes as it melted in my mouth. Nothing had ever tasted so good. Alfie and Eliza would love these. I picked out another two to take back for them and then Dembow closed the box. Just as he was putting it back in the cupboard, there was a sudden noise. A bang from overhead – like a door closing – and I jumped. The chocolate I was eating stuck in the back of my throat and I began to choke. I coughed. I couldn't help it. But Dembow grabbed hold of me and whacked me on the back, sending the chocolate shooting across the floor.

'Shhh!' he said, holding his hand across my mouth to deaden the sound of my coughing. When I managed to stop, we waited to see if anyone had heard us. Nobody came, so I picked up the chocolate, wiped it on my sleeve and ate it. Didn't want to waste it, see.

Dembow put the box back and I don't suppose the Mogwurts would ever notice some chocolates were missing.

After the parlour, we crept down the corridor and into the dining room where, a few hours earlier, we had eaten the rabbit pie. The table was clear now and polished so the wood shone like a mirror. But I was worried about Ma's box. Missus Mugwort had put it on the sideboard, which had been cleaned and polished just like the table. But it was gone.

I tapped Dembow on the shoulder and mouthed the word 'box' and he seemed to understand. He tugged my arm and leaned close so that he could whisper in my ear. 'I know plenty of other places they could have put it. Don't worry.'

He walked round the table to the sideboard which had two small cupboards and he began to undo the locks with his bit of wire. Both of them were crammed with all kinds of stuff: silver knives, forks and spoons, drinking goblets, cruet sets, linen napkins... things I'd never seen before. But the clothes weren't there. I was beginning to wonder if we'd ever find them or whether we should run away in our shirts.

Dembow locked the cupboard doors with his bit of wire and then he pointed up to the ceiling. I wanted to ask him what he meant – but I couldn't make a noise, see. He nodded towards the door, expecting me to follow him. It wasn't until we reached the bottom of the stairs that I realised he was taking me to the Mogwurts' bedroom. Well, I ask you!

I wanted to yell, 'NO! TOO DANGEROUS!' Instead I grabbed hold of his shirt so that he turned round. Then I shook my head violently and mouthed, 'We can't!' But Dembow pushed my hand away and began to climb. Like a stupe, I followed. This was mad. With every step, the stairs creaked and groaned, even though we went up very, very slowly. And the noise echoed through the house.

By the time we reached the landing, my heart was banging fit to burst. The Mogwurts were sure to hear. Any minute they'd catch us. But as we reached to top, I could hear snoring coming from the bedroom. One snore was high and twittering with a sort of whistling sound – which must have been Missus Mogwurt. The other was Mister Mogwurt – deep and grunting like a pig. Every now and then he would stop with a splutter and start again a second later with a long snort. The Mogwurts were definitely asleep.

Thirty-Four

The Mogwurts' bedroom

On the landing by the bedroom door was a large oak chest with a padlock on the front. Like everything in Blythwell Hall, it was locked. Dembow looked at me and winked before bending down and pushing his piece of wire and twiddling it this way and that until the lock sprang open.

When he lifted the lid, I held the candle over the chest so that we could see what was in there. It was packed full of stuff and, right at the top, were our clothes. Alfie's trousers, Eliza's skirt, my new jacket. Everything that Missus Mogwurt had taken was lying there folded as neat as you please. And – love a duck! – the boots were there, too, clean and polished so you could see your face in 'em.

I started to take them out of the chest but Dembow shook his head and mouthed, 'The box.' I'd been so glad to find the clothes that I'd forgotten Ma's box. But Dembow hadn't. He wanted to find it before we unloaded the clothes.

He pointed to the door behind us, went to turn the doorknob and slowly pushed it open. Was he mad? I thought. The Mogwurts were in that room. It was like going into a lion's den! We were sure to get caught.

But Dembow tiptoed in and I followed, didn't I? I was carrying that candle and shaking like fool, not knowing what would happen next.

The first shock I had was the bedroom. I ain't never seen such a room. It was enormous. You could have had a game of cricket in there, I tell you. There was a great mahogany bed opposite the door and, lying on it like two whales washed up on a beach, were the Mogwurts. They were covered in a blue eiderdown, with their hands folded over their bellies and their heads topped with nightcaps. I wanted to laugh out loud.

Near to the door was a dressing table and a neat little stool, all ladylike for Missus Mogwurt. There was a silver-backed hair brush on the dressing table and next to it was a heap of black hair which I realised was Missus Mogwurt's wig. I nudged Dembow and pointed to it. This time I couldn't control myself, and I nearly died laughing, putting my hand over my mouth so I didn't make a noise.

When I'd calmed down, I started to look about for the box, but Dembow was obviously having fun. He tiptoed over to the dressing table, picked up the wig and put it on his head for a joke. That was when I spotted something glinting in the shadows of the room. Hidden under the wig was Ma's silver box.

I pointed to it and Dembow passed it to me before stuffing the wig in his pocket. Now we could get out of here! I turned to leave the room, but he beckoned me to follow him over to a wardrobe next to one of the tall windows, covered with red velvet curtains. Dembow opened the wardrobe doors and shut them again. Then he took out his wire and turned it in the locks. This was a daft thing to do, I thought. Why would he want to lock the wardrobe? But I couldn't ask him, see.

Then, the worst thing happened. On the other side of the bedroom, Mister Mogwurt began to stir in his bed. He muttered, 'What? What?' before he turned onto his side, flung his arm on top of his wife who also began to stir. The Mogwurts were waking up.

Lawks! We're done for, I thought, and quickly blew out the candle. Dembow grabbed hold of my arm and pulled me behind the velvet curtains. We stood there without moving a muscle, my heart thumping against my ribs, while Mister Mogwurt made some odd grumbling noises. 'Humph! What? Grunt.' And his wife said, 'Quiet, Mogwurt, you foolish man.'

I heard them tossing and turning and I thought I'd faint clean away I was that scared.

Then suddenly Missus Mogwurt said, 'A noise, Mogwurt. I heard a noise.'

Mister Mogwurt groaned.

'Listen!' she barked. 'Wake up, husband!'

The bed springs creaked as Mister Mogwurt slowly sat up. 'It's nothing, dear. Just an owl hooting,' he said and flopped down again.

'Nothing?' yelled Missus Mogwurt, whacking her husband with the back of her hand. 'My ears are sharp as pins. I heard something, I tell you. Get up and take a look.'

'I don't think—'

'Go!' said his wife. Then came a loud thump on the floor, and I guessed she'd shoved him out of bed.

'Go onto the landing,' she bellowed. 'And go downstairs and check the front door is locked and bolted.'

Mister Mogwurt struck a match and lit the candle by his bed. My heart was pounding in my ears as I flattened myself against the window behind the curtain. Dembow gripped my arm and we both held our breath as we stood watching the shadows flicker and listening to Mogwurt's footsteps cross over to the door and out onto the landing. Then a question came into my head. Did we close the lid of the chest? Or did we leave it open? I tried to remember but I couldn't. If we hadn't shut it, we were done for. He would know somebody was about.

After what felt like hours, I heard him coming back and Mogwurt's footsteps came back into the bedroom.

'All clear, dear,' he said. 'It must have been the wind. You can go back to sleep.'

'Are you sure, husband? Have you checked everywhere?'

'All checked,' he said, blowing out the light and climbing back into bed.

Lawks! Would they fall asleep now? How long would we have to wait? I heard the Mogwurts settle themselves in the bed and tug at the quilt. Then they began to breathe heavily and, after some time, they began to snore again.

As soon as we were sure they were sleeping soundly, we crawled from under the curtains on hands and knees and over to the door. With only the smallest of creaking, I managed to pull it open and then went out onto the landing. What an escape, eh? I took the biggest breath!

We hurried to the chest and unpacked the clothes. Then we each carried a pile and slung the boots round our necks with their laces tied together to make our way back to Eliza and Alfie.

As you might expect, they were real glad to see us.

'My boots!' Alfie cried.

'You got the box!' squealed Eliza.

Dembow put his finger to his lips. 'Keep yer voices down,' he hissed. 'Don't want Smidgeby to hear, do yer?'

I soon sorted out the clothes. I helped Alfie into his jacket and Eliza picked her grey wool skirt off the pile and put it on. 'You done well, Sam,' she whispered. 'It'll be jammy to be warm again.'

We got dressed in double-quick time.

'Can we go to Grandpa's house now then?' Alfie asked as he tried to tie his laces. 'He's going to look after us, ain't he?'

'Course he is,' Dembow answered. 'You'll have to get out of here sharpish before Smidgeby gets up.'

'But it's pitch-black outside,' Eliza said. 'We'll never find our way.'

Dembow nodded. 'I've thought of that. You can hide in the garden till it gets light. But listen! If you hears anything – shoutin' or argufyin' or that – it might mean they've found out you've gone, see, and they'll come lookin'. You gotta scarper, even in the dark. It's your only chance.'

'I remember that big tree in front of the house,' I said. 'We can hide there. Nobody will see us.'

Before we left, I checked that our letters were in the box and then I tucked it inside my jacket. We stepped out into the corridor and Dembow turned the wire in the keyhole to lock the door behind us. Smidgeby would have a surprise in the morning when he found us gone!

With Patch on his rope lead, we crept down the passageway until we came to the front door. Dembow turned to look at us and put his finger to his lips. Then he bent forward and gripped the bolt, tugging it a bit at a time, while we hopped about nervously until it slipped from the metal bars. He pulled back another bolt without any trouble and then he took hold of the iron key in the keyhole and turned it until it clicked open. It was done.

Dembow grinned as he opened the door and let us through. 'Good luck with the old geezer,' he whispered. 'Tell your grandpa about us. Don't forget, will yer?'

I grasped Dembow's hand in thanks for what he'd done. Then we ran out of that terrible place and into the cold night.

Thirty-Five

The wind and a nightcap

The night was black as tar. The rain was coming down in stair-rods as we found our way to the cedar tree. Its drooping branches sheltered us from the worst of it but it was a long time till morning and we huddled together as the night got colder and colder. The rain didn't stop and soon it began to drip through the branches.

Just a glimmer of light – that's all we needed – and we could be on our way.

Suddenly Patch tugged on his rope and started barking.

'Stow it, Patch!' I whispered, grabbing hold of him and tucking him under my arm to shut him up.

But then we heard a terrible noise – banging and screaming and shouting – coming from the house.

'What's that?' asked Eliza.

'Cripes!' I said. 'The Mogwurts must have found out we got away.'

She grabbed hold of my sleeve. 'We ain't safe here, Sam. Let's run for it before the old witch comes looking for us.'

'But it's pitch black, there ain't no moon tonight,' I said. 'We'll never find the gate in time. We could be running round in circles, girl.' I thought for a minute and then it came to me. 'We'll climb the tree. It'll be just like the old days. They won't see us up in the branches.'

Without a word, Eliza and Alfie scrambled up the trunk. Even though their hands were slipping on the wet bark, they managed it. Eliza was just as good as she always was, and they shuffled onto a thick bough. I passed Patch up to Eliza before I started the climb myself. Then we sat side by side like crows in the night. Waiting. Wondering if we'd be found.

By the time we were all settled, the shouting from the house had died down.

'They're not coming!' said Eliza. 'They've searched the house and they ain't found nothing. I bet they've gone back to bed. We're safe, ain't we, Sam?'

She was hoping that was the end of it, but I thought different, see. I knew they'd come out looking for us.

I peered through the branches, and it wasn't long before I saw the front door open and the light from two oil lamps spilled out across the grass.

'They're here,' I hissed. 'Stay as still as you can.' And we gripped the branch tighter than ever.

Scared as I was, the sight of the Mogwurts on that rainy night made me want to laugh. Now I knew why Dembow had locked that wardrobe. They'd no clothes to put on over their nightshirts. They'd no shoes, neither. They stood in the doorway with blankets round their shoulders and nightcaps on their heads, looking like real dopes.

'Go and find them wicked children!' screamed Missus

Mogwurt as the rain beat down heavier than ever. 'Don't let 'em get away, husband. They's worth a fortune to us. Get out there and find 'em!'

He stepped outside in his bare feet, holding his lamp high, looking this way and that. But it was dark out there and the rain was heavy. I don't suppose he could see very far.

Missus Mogwurt was in a right temper and she didn't wait for long before she went after him, head down again the rain. 'Don't just stand there, Mogwurt. Go looking!' she shouted and prodded him so hard in the back that he slipped on a patch of mud. Oh lawks! He went skidding over the ground with his arms circling like a windmill. He tried to keep his balance but he couldn't and landed flat on his back.

'Get up, you great stupe,' yelled Missus Mogwurt, but her husband couldn't get up on account of his large belly, so she had to step into the mud to help him.

She was bending over pulling on his arm when a sudden gust of wind snatched the cap from her head leaving her bald as a hen's egg. She screamed, 'Aaaaghhh!' when the cap was tossed it into the air and she leaped to catch it. Then the blanket fell from her shoulders into the mud and she was left standing in nothing but her nightgown.

Eliza and me laughed, and Alfie giggled so much I was worried he'd fall out of the tree.

But that wasn't the end of it. When the wind dropped, the cap fell back to earth. Missus Mogwurt scrambled after it and went slipping and sliding until she fell face down. And when she lifted her head, she saw the cap being tossed and blown across the garden till it landed up in the branches of a big tree where it got stuck.

By then she covered in mud and angry as a bull on market day. She scrambled to her feet and pulled the blanket over her head to hide her baldness. Then she dragged herself over to her husband who was now kneeling on all fours still trying to get onto his feet.

We were all rocking with laughter. We couldn't help it. We'd never seen anything like it.

'You stupid man!' the old witch screamed. 'Fetch my cap. Fetch it, Mister Mogwurt!' But it was obvious that the mud-soaked cove couldn't reach it. So she swung her clenched fist at him and gave him a real good thumping before she stomped back into the house.

'I can't hold on much longer, Sam,' said Alfie once we'd stopped laughing. 'I'm going to fall.'

'Five more minutes,' I whispered and put my arm round him. 'Then we can get down.'

When the five minutes were up and we about to climb down the tree, the front door opened again.

'Don't move,' I snapped. 'They're back.'

This time it wasn't just the Mogwurts. All the children what lived there came as well. They came running out into the driving rain, bare-footed and dressed in them terrible thin clothes.

Smidgeby and the Mogwurts stayed dry in the doorway. Missus M was holding a lamp and clutching a clean blanket over her baldness while she yelled at the children. 'Search every corner, you dunderheads. You'll go without food if you don't find them varmints.'

The poor things must have been terrified. They spread out over the grass like a swarm of ants, treading through the shrubs and searching every possible hiding place.

We watched them – though Alfie was too frightened to look and squeezed his eyes shut. I thought no one would see us perched up high. But I was wrong. One of them was running towards our tree.

'Not a sound, Alfie,' I whispered and hugged him tight while Eliza clapped her hand over Patch's mouth in case he barked.

The black shadow of a boy pushed his way through the branches and into the space around the trunk. If he looked up, he'd see us for sure. We clung onto the tree, terrified. The boy glanced around the trunk and, just when I thought he might go, he looked up. The game was over.

'Don't you say a word,' he hissed, 'or you're done for.'

We stared down through the gloom.

Then Eliza chuckled under her breath. 'Dembow?' she called softly. 'That's you, ain't it?'

'Yeah! Who d'you think?' he whispered. 'You stay here and I'll see you right.' And with that he ran away, calling, 'They ain't here, Missus Mogwurt.' Then he pointed to the far side of the garden. 'Over there! Look! That's them. They're gettin' away over the wall.'

There was a great commotion when Missus Mogwurt ran out into the rain, clutching the blanket and flinging her arms about screaming, 'The wall! The wall! Go and climb over it.' And though the poor things did their best, there were too many of 'em and they bumped into each other and landed in a heap on the ground.

Missus Mogwurt was wild with rage, thinking we was getting away. She pointed in different directions. 'Over there! No, no. That way, stupid boy.' And she ran about, this way and that, like a chicken in a coop and we couldn't help laughing.

She didn't give up till every part of the garden had been searched. Then she threw up her mud-covered hands in despair, moaning, 'GAWN! They've gawn!' before swooning into Mister Mogwurt's arms.

Thirty-Six

On to Blythfield Hall

As soon as the Mogwurts were back inside, we slithered down the tree trunk. The rain was worse than ever but we couldn't stay. I had to get us out of that garden somehow. In the dark, we stumbled over the grass and managed to find the drive which was rough with stones and broken branches. It wasn't easy. Alfie had started coughing and I was worried he was like to get a chill. We tripped up several times and once Eliza fell headlong and hurt herself.

I picked her up. 'You all right?' I asked.

'No, I ain't,' she sobbed. 'My new skirt got ripped. It's got a big hole in it.'

She was that upset about her skirt, it didn't seem to matter that her knee was bleeding and she couldn't walk proper. That's girls for you!

By the time we reached the gates we were soaked to the skin. But we sheltered against the wall and waited for daylight so we could see our way.

Alfie didn't understand. 'When will we get to Grandpa's?' he wailed. But I couldn't give him an answer.

At last, the rain turned to a drizzle and the sky changed

from darkest black to grey.

'It's light enough now, ain't it, Sam?' said Eliza.

'What about your knee?'

'It ain't so bad. I can walk well enough.'

The light was still dim but I could see the lane and the hedges on either side.

'Let's get moving,' I said. 'Next stop Blythfield Hall.'

But walking wasn't easy. The rain had turned the ground into a right muddy mess. Our boots sank deep and the effort of pulling them out made our legs ache something shocking. I could see Alfie was suffering in another way. His cough was getting worse and his face was flushed pink as if he was burning up with fever.

'I'm tired,' he said and I knew his little legs had grown weak so he could hardly put one foot in front of the other. There was nothing for it but to carry him.

When we came to the signpost we'd seen on the way to Blythwell Hall, Eliza got all excited.

'This is it,' said Eliza, pushing her dripping hair out of her eyes. 'This is where we gone wrong before. We should have turned up here, I reckon. Mister Mogwurt said Grandpa's house was at the top of a hill, didn't he?'

'Naw!' I said. 'A toff wouldn't live there? You couldn't get a carriage up that lane, could yer? It ain't wide enough.'

Eliza was in a real mood ever since she'd torn her skirt. 'That's what you think, is it?' she snapped. 'Well go and look at that signpost.'

Just to please her, I did. The wood was old and rotten but,

even in the dim light, I managed to make out the words carved on it. 'You're right, sis,' I said. 'This is the way to Blythfield Hall.'

A signpost can't lie, can it? So we all set off, bursting with excitement like it was Christmas and birthdays rolled into one. By the time we reached the top of the hill, the rain had stopped altogether. A watery, winter sun broke through the clouds and we could see ahead for a mile or so. Best of all, at the top of a bank was a big house, with tall windows looking out across the countryside.

'Didn't I tell yer?' said Eliza, looking very pleased with herself. 'That's it. That's Grandpa's house. I'm certain sure.' She skipped ahead and, if I hadn't been carrying Alfie, I'd have skipped too. After all that had happened, I was feeling real chirpy.

The house was a fine one built of stone. Over the front door was a portico with four pillars where a carriage could pull up so that grand ladies or gentlemen could get out and walk in to the house without getting wet.

'Oh, ain't it exciting?' said Eliza as we stood staring at the huge front door.

'Go on,' I said. 'You knock, Eliza.'

She grinned at me and reached up for the brass knocker with a lion's head. She hammered onto the door so that it made a noise like thunder. Everybody in the house must have heard it and soon there were footsteps marching down the hall. Then the door opened and a man dressed from head to toe in black stood there staring at Eliza.

She stepped forward as bold as you like and smiled at him.

'I'm Eliza,' she said, 'and these are my brothers Sam and Alfie – only Alfie ain't very well, see, on account of getting soaking wet. We've come a long way especially to see you.' But the man was frowning and looked quite angry. So Eliza took a deep breath and said, 'Are you our grandfather?'

The man raised his eyebrows, looked down his nose at her and said, 'No, I am certainly not your grandfather.'

He was about to shut the door when I said, 'Excuse me, sir. My sister don't know nothing.'

Then I turned to Eliza. 'He ain't our grandpa, stupe. He's a butler. Toffs don't answer their own front door, do they?'

I slipped Alfie off my shoulder and sat him on the step. But the butler seemed very annoyed at the sight of us. I don't know why. Could we help it if we were soaked through and splashed with a bit of mud? Could we help it if Patch barked at him? If you ask me, some people are just plain miserable. Always are. Always will be. But it did cross my mind that we might not be welcome.

'Go away,' he said in a deep voice that was a bit on the scary side. 'Beggars are not allowed here. Go and beg somewhere else.'

He tried to close the door but I held out my hand and stopped him.

'We wasn't begging, sir. We was looking for Sir Samuel Pargeter. We're his grandchildren, see.'

The butler sniffed. 'Really?' he said. 'And why would you come now? Sir Samuel is dead.' And with that, he slammed the door in our faces.

Thirty-Seven

The cook and the maid

None of us spoke for a minute or so. We were stunned by the news. I leaned against the stone pillar as thoughts of the past few days fizzed around in my head. We'd searched for Grandpa's address and been thrown into prison. We'd travelled on that terrible train to get here, then been kidnapped by the Mugworts. What was it for, eh? We'd come all this way and he wasn't here. He was dead. Now we'd never see him.

'Well,' Eliza said, brushing away a tear. 'That's a terrible thing Grandpa dying like that. But that butler ain't got no manners, has he? Speaking to us like that.'

I bent down to pick up Alfie who was curled up and shivering on the stone slab. 'Come on little un. We've got to go,' I said – though I didn't know where we could go to. I stood with Alfie in my arms remembering what Pa had said to me. 'While I'm away, Sam, I want you to look after Ma and your sister and brother. Can you manage that?' But I hadn't managed it, had I? I'd failed.

Eliza had other ideas. 'I'm thinking,' she said. 'Why don't we go round the back. See if there's a maid or something who'll tell us what happened to our grandpa. She might be kind and give us something to eat, eh? Just as long as that that snoot of a butler don't see us.'

It was better than nothing, I suppose. She held Patch's rope and I carried Alfie as we hurried past the front of the house and round the corner. There we found another door, much smaller with three narrow stone steps leading up to it. We couldn't see a bell or a knocker, so Eliza balled her fist and banged on the door as loudly as she could.

It was opened by a stout lady in a white apron and cap with hands covered in flour and a great white splodge on her nose.

'Well?' she said, wiping her hands on her apron. 'What do you little beggars want?'

No sooner had she spoken than a young woman in a black dress and a white cap appeared behind her, looking over her shoulder.

'Oh, poor things. They look hungry, Missus O'Leary,' she said, giving us a lovely, friendly smile. 'They need feeding, for sure.'

'Hungry they may be, Bridget, but you know the mistress's nerves are in a terrible state these days. She don't like people coming to the house.'

'Ah, but they're only young, Missus O. It wouldn't do any harm to give 'em a crust, would it? They're as thin as sticks and the nipper don't look at all well, does he?'

'He's not well,' I cut in. 'Please, missus, can we come in for just a minute?'

'Certainly not,' said Missus O'Leary and returned to the kitchen while Bridget bent down to stroke Patch. 'Cook's all right, really,' she whispered. 'Her bark's worse that her bite. She'll find you something to eat – so don't you worry yourselves.'

'Well, we are worried,' said Eliza. 'We've come to visit our grandpa, see.'

I nodded and looked at Bridget. I knew she was the kind of person who would understand.

'Your grandfather? Is that so?' said Bridget standing up and folding her arms across her chest. 'And does this grandfather of yours have a name?'

'Sir Samuel Pargeter,' I said, 'but we've never met him.'

She stared, her eyes growing as big as dinner plates. 'Sir Samuel! Well, I never. Did you hear that Missus O'Leary?' she called over her shoulder. 'These are Sir Samuel's grandchildren. Have you ever heard the like?'

The cook returned carrying a small loaf of bread.

'I heard what the child said, Bridget. She certainly knows how to tell a story, does she not?' she said, wagging her finger at Eliza. 'Show some respect, girl. Sir Samuel died but three weeks ago and the house is in mourning. Be off with you. Leave poor Lady Margaret in peace.'

'Lady Margaret? Is she Sir Samuel's wife, missus?' I asked the cook.

'And what if she is?'

'I've got a letter what our aunt wrote to Sir Samuel, see. I reckon she'll be interested in seeing it.' I set Alfie on the step and pulled the silver box from inside my jacket. Then I took out the letter and offered it to Missus O'Leary. But she pushed it

211

away. 'I have no wish to see your letter and neither will Lady Margaret. Now get away!' she said and marched back into the house, making a grunting noise like a bad tempered pig.

I could tell Bridget felt sorry for us. 'Let me see what you've got,' she whispered and took the letter from me.

'It's from our Aunt Maud what used to look after us,' Eliza explained. 'It's got our grandpa's address on the front, see.'

Bridget unfolded the paper and, as she read it, she pressed her fingers to her mouth. 'Oh, Heaven preserve us! Who would have thought it?' Then, with the letter clutched to her chest, she looked at us. 'If this letter is right, Lady Margaret is your grandma. She'll be wanting to see this, for sure. Stay here and I'll be back to tell you what she says.'

Thirty-Eight

Lady Margaret

Bridget tucked the letter into the pocket of her white apron and went back into the kitchen.

'Did you get rid of them kids?' we heard Missus O'Leary say. 'Can't be doing with beggars. I've no time for 'em.'

Bridget laughed. 'Sure, they're just children,' she said, 'and poor ones at that.'

'Well, that's as maybe,' replied the cook. 'Now take the mistress's breakfast and hurry up. It's five minutes late already.'

We sat on the steps outside the kitchen to eat the bread. Eliza settled the nipper on her knee and wrapped her shawl round him trying to keep him warm. Patch wouldn't leave him. I think he knew Alfie wasn't well. The three of us clung together and, when we'd finished eating, Eliza sang 'Twinkle Twinkle Little Star', hoping it would make Alfie feel better.

All this time we were waiting for Bridget to come back and when she finally opened the kitchen door I was shocked to see that her eyes were red from crying.

'What happened?' I asked.

She tried to sniff away her tears. 'I did my best,' she said.

'I gave Lady Margaret the letter but...' she broke out into sobs and couldn't continue.

'Don't upset yourself, Bridget,' said Eliza, putting Alfie on the step where he lolled against the wall, fast asleep. 'Just tell us what happened.'

Bridget nodded and wiped her cheeks. 'I gave the letter to Lady Margaret and she wouldn't even read it. She just pushed it away. But I had to make her listen. She needed to know that you were her grandchildren, didn't she? So I read it out loud.'

'Then what?'

'Oh, she got into a terrible temper. She said I was a foolish girl. Weak in the head. She said that and anybody could have written that letter. It was a fraud.'

'A fraud?' I said. 'How could she think that?'

'I don't know,' Bridget sobbed. 'I've worked at Blythfield Hall for three years with never a cross word. I know Lady Margaret's been upset since Sir Samuel died – but she was in such a rage. She told me to leave the house and now I'm dismissed from her service. I've no work and nowhere to go.' Tears spilled onto her cheeks and ran down to her chin. Poor Bridget! Now she'd got no job – just because she was trying to help us.

'Did you tell Missus O'Leary what happened?' asked Eliza.

'She's not here. I expect she's down the cellar,' Bridget sniffed. 'But I don't suppose she can do anything. Lady Margaret won't listen to her.'

She sank onto the step, her head in her hands.

'Well,' said Eliza, 'we ain't going to put up with that, eh,

Sam? We'll go and tell Lady Margaret that letter's no fraud and that you're no stupe.'

'Right! We'll do that,' I said and lifted Alfie onto my shoulder. 'Just tell us where to find her, will yer, Bridget?'

'Well, I s'pose I haven't got nothing to lose,' she said. 'Straight through the kitchen and down the passageway. The dining room's the first door on the right.'

We left Bridget sitting on the step and walked through the kitchen on our way to find Lady Margaret.

Alfie opened his eyes. 'Can I see Grandpa?' he wailed, barely awake.

'We're in his house, little un,' said Eliza, leading the way with Patch. 'You be a good boy. Everything will be all right.'

We turned a corner into the large entrance hall and found the door to the dining room was on the right, just as Bridget said. I took hold of Eliza's arm and held her back, taking deep breaths to calm our nerves. Then I knocked at the door and, without waiting for an answer, opened it and we marched in with Patch following behind.

The sight took my breath away. The room was huge with high windows and fancy curtains. Sitting at the far end of a mahogany table was an old woman dressed in black with white hair pulled back from her face. Lady Margaret was having her breakfast. As we walked in, she paused with a forkful of scrambled egg halfway to her mouth and stared as if she had never seen anything like us in her life.

Eliza didn't wait for her to speak. She went right up to her and said, 'Excuse us, madam. I'm sorry to disturb you, but we was wondering if you was Lady Margaret Pargeter? Cos if so, then you're our grandma. But we ain't never seen you before.'

Lady Margaret dropped her fork onto her plate and glared, her mouth open with the shock of it. I suppose we did look wet and muddy and I don't suppose she'd ever had a dog stand on her fine carpet before. Still, she might have said something. Made us feel welcome. But she didn't. Not one word. So I took up the conversation.

'This is my sister, Eliza,' I said, as polite as you like. 'This is Alfie on my shoulder here. He ain't very well as you can see. And this is our dog, Patch, and I'm Sam. Named after Sir Samuel, I was. Our father named me after him.'

Still she didn't speak. Instead, she reached for a small brass bell on the table and rang it. 'Wetherby!' she called. 'Wetherby! Come at once!'

The butler — him with the shocking manners — came rushing into the dining room, pulling on his black jacket and smoothing his hair. But when he caught sight of us by the table, his face went pale..

'I b-beg your pardon, madam,' he stuttered. 'These beggars came to the front door earlier this morning and I assure you that I sent them away. I don't know how they came to enter the house, madam. I'll get rid of them at once.'

'See to it,' said Lady Margaret who turned back to her breakfast and took a mouthful of scrambled egg.

Wetherby marched towards us looking as fierce as any bruiser in a boxing ring. Was he going to beat us or drag us away? All I knew was that I was scared stiff. And I wasn't

216

the only one. Patch got all agitated too, and started to growl. But the butler took no notice, thinking the dog was too small to do any harm, see. He reached out to grab hold of Eliza.

'Leave me alone!' she yelled and let go of Patch's rope. Once he was free to leap at Wetherby, he sank his sharp little teeth into his ankle and the butler set up such a wailing and a hollering as you've ever heard.

'*Aaaagh!* Get him off!' he yelled. Then Patch, being a polite sort of dog, let go. But he stood there, fixing him with his dark, button eyes. Every time the butler tried to step forward, Patch bared his teeth as a warning.

Lady Margaret stood up to protest, but Wetherby said, 'Stay where you are, madam. This dog is dangerous. Don't come near.' And the old woman slumped back into her chair.

'Sorry about Patch, madam,' said Eliza, 'but he's just looking after us, see. We only wanted to talk to you and show you our letters.'

'I've seen your letter,' Lady Margaret replied and put her hand to her forehead like she'd got a terrible headache. 'The maid showed it to me. The silly girl believed what it said. But I'm not easily fooled, child.' Then she looked up at Eliza. 'Anyone could have written that. I expect you think I'll give you money, don't you? Well, I won't and that's that!'

Somehow, I had to make her believe us. I lifted Alfie off my shoulder and sat him on one of the dining chairs. Then I set the silver box on the table, took the letters out and placed them in front of her. 'That first letter was from our aunt. But

217

I've got two more here. If I gives 'em to you, will you read 'em?'

But Lady Margaret wasn't listening. She was staring at the silver box. 'I know that box. Where did you get it?' she snapped. 'Did you steal it, boy?'

I was furious. 'I ain't no thief. Our pa gave it to our ma when they was married. It's very old that is. It belonged to Pa's grandma, he told us once. It's special, see.'

Lady Margaret's hand was trembling as she touched her cheek. 'And where did you hear that story? Tell me the truth. How did you come by that box?'

'It's the truth, I tell yer. Just read them letters and you'll see,' I said as another growl came from Patch. 'If you'll be so kind as to look at the letters, I could call the dog off.'

Seeing that it was the only way to end this situation, Lady Margaret shugged her shoulders and said, 'Very well. If it means that you will go away...'

I leaned over the table, pointing at the letter. 'Our pa wrote that one to our ma,' I explained. 'That was more than two years ago.'

'He went to foreign parts to find work, see,' said Eliza. 'He never come back, though. And then Ma died and our Aunt Maud looked after us and we don't know where he is or if—'

Lady Margaret held her hand up for silence as she picked up the creased and yellowed letters. Her mouth was fixed tight as she bent over to read them. But her expression softened and after she'd finished reading all three, her eyes were wet with tears.

'You believe us now, don't yer?' I said as the lady wiped her cheeks with her handkerchief. 'We told you we was your grandchildren. No lies, eh?'

But when Lady Margaret raised her head, her face was full of anger. 'How dare you?' she shrieked and got to her feet, waving the papers in my face. 'Where did you get these, boy?'

'What do you mean?' I asked.

'This is my son's handwriting. I'd know it anywhere. Did you steal the letters, you rogue? Tell me now or I shall send for the constable.'

Thirty-Nine

A doctor and a patient

All this time, Alfie was sitting on the chair, watching. When the old lady stood up, he thought she was going to hit me, see. So he slid off the chair and tried to stop the quarrel. He shouted, 'No! Don't touch him!' but his poor little legs were too weak to stand. His knees buckled under him and he collapsed on the floor and lay there stock still.

Patch left the butler and raced over, licking the nipper's face, hoping he would wake up. But Alfie didn't move. Eliza and me kneeled beside him and patted his cheeks, which were flushed red.

'Alfie!' I said and shook his arm gently and wiped the beads of sweat from his forehead. 'Nipper! Come on. Wake up.' But he didn't open his eyes and I felt helpless.

Lady Margaret rang the little bell again. 'Missus O'Leary!' she called. 'Missus O'Leary.'

'I'll go and fetch her, madam,' said Wetherby, straightening his jacket. 'She might not have heard.'

But before he had reached the door, Missus O'Leary came bustling in, followed by Bridget.

'Whatever is it, madam? What's happened?' When she saw

the group of us crowded round Alfie, she said, 'Well, I'm blowed! It's them beggars!'

'I fear this child is sick, Missus O'Leary. What are we going to do?'

Bridget pushed her way forward and looked at Alfie. 'Begging your pardon, madam, but he's got a fever. He's a poor thing. Just look at him.'

Missus O'Leary shook her head. 'He's like to die,' she said. 'My brother looked just like that and he was dead within the week.'

'Don't talk like that!' Eliza said taking Alfie in her arms. 'He ain't going to die. He's cold and wet, that's all. He needs a home, he does, and somebody to take care of him.' And she rocked him backwards and forward and started to sing 'Twinkle, Twinkle, Little Star' again.

Not knowing what else to do, we all stood and listened to Eliza's sweet voice.

'He likes that song,' I whispered to Lady Margaret. 'He likes our Eliza to sing to him when he ain't feeling so good.'

I was surprised when the old lady suddenly waved to the butler. 'Fetch the doctor, Wetherby. Let us see if he can do anything to help.'

In less than five minutes, a doctor came hurrying into the room. It was like magic. Where he came from, I didn't know. I swear that's the truth. He just suddenly appeared. He told Bridget to fetch a blanket and asked us all to step away while he examined his patient.

Eliza was still holding Alfie and the doctor put his hand on her shoulder. 'Don't stop singing, my dear,' he said. 'You stay there. Your lovely voice will be a comfort to your little brother.'

He kneeled down to examine Alfie while Missus O'Leary went to boil some water in case it was needed. I fretted and paced up and down waiting to see what the doctor could do. And all the time Eliza kept singing.

It was then that Lady Margaret suddenly hurried over to the doorway and I heard her say, 'You shouldn't have come downstairs,' sounding all anxious like. I glanced up to see a man standing in the doorway. He was wearing a dressing gown and leaning heavily on a stick. His face was pale under his bushy beard and he looked so thin and weak that I was surprised he could stand at all.

The pale man didn't look at Lady Margaret, instead his eyes flickered round the room. 'That voice,' he said. 'That's my Annie's voice. Where is she? Is she here?'

'Come,' said the old lady, leading him to a chair. 'Sit down, my dear. You're dreaming. You're not fully recovered yet.'

The doctor looked up and smiled. 'It's a good sign, Lady Margaret. He's managed to walk down the stairs after lying in bed these past weeks. You'll see your son's health improve now, I promise you.'

I wondered if I'd heard right. Was this sickly man Lady Margaret's son? That would make him Pa's brother – though I never knew he had one.

I went over to where he was sitting. 'Sir,' I said. 'Are you our uncle? I'm Sam and that's Eliza over there singing to our Alfie.'

The man stared at me with wild eyes before looking over at Eliza. Then he gripped the edge of the table as if he was near to fainting.

'No!' he said in a voice so quiet that I could hardly hear him. 'I am not your uncle.' Then he suddenly wrapped his arms around me and pulled me close to his chest. 'I am your father, my dear boy. It's me – I'm your very own pa.' And he began to weep.

Forty

Our family together at last

Everything happened so fast after that, I can scarcely remember it all. But I'll do my best.

Pa was swaying, hardly able to stand. But he looked at Lady Margaret and said, 'This boy is my son, Mother. And over there are my younger son and my daughter. Please help me across to them.'

Lady Margaret could hardly speak. It must have been a terrible shock for her. But I could see she was glad that Pa was on the mend and, once she got used to the idea, I think she was glad to have grandchildren.

She put her arm round Pa to support him. Then Pa put his arm on my shoulder and the three of us walked slowly together across the room until we reached Eliza who was still sitting on the floor, singing to Alfie.

Pa reached out his hand and rested it gently on her head. 'Eliza, my dear girl, you have the voice of your mother,' he said and she stopped singing and looked up at him. 'You have grown but I would know that red hair and that beautiful voice anywhere.'

She stared, but I could tell that she didn't recognise him.

It had been so long since we had seen him and he was so changed. So thin. So pale.

'It's Pa, stupe!' I said.

Eliza blinked, not believing what I'd said.

'Don't just sit there. It's true.'

Then, as if it suddenly dawned on her, she jumped up like a crazy girl and flung herself at him, beating his chest with her fists. 'We thought you was dead! We thought you was dead!' she screamed. Then she wrapped her arms round his waist and sobbed liked a baby.

There were gasps and oohs and aaahs. Pa told everybody in that room that we were his children. It must have been hard for him seeing us dirty like that – looking like beggars. But it didn't stop him from hugging us, going from me to Eliza and back again.

When Alfie finally opened his eyes, we were so pleased that we all cheered. The nipper must have been puzzled seeing people standing round him.

'Where's my grandpa?' he said in a weak little voice. 'Sam, is he here?'

Lady Margaret kneeled by his side and smiled. 'I am your grandmother, my child. You are safe now and your pa is with you.'

It was all too much for Alfie who must have thought it was a dream. He looked up at Grandma, smiled and went back to sleep.

'The boy will soon recover with dry clothes and good food,' said the doctor. 'There's a cut to his foot that is badly infected and must be cared for. I have some cream in my bag.'

'I'll see to that,' said Missus O'Leary, taking the jar. 'And Bridget can help.'

The doctor nodded and turned to Lady Margaret. 'Now your son must go back to bed, madam.'

Pa shook his head. 'I want to be with my children. I have been apart from them for so long.'

'Later.' The doctor was firm. 'They will still be here this evening. Until then, their grandmother will take care of them.'

We gave Pa a hug and the doctor helped him up the stairs to rest for a while.

Once he had gone, Grandma asked Missus O'Leary to bring breakfast for us. 'I remember your father was always hungry at your age,' she told us. And soon steaming plates of porridge were brought into the dining room and later a tray full of chops and kidneys and bacon was carried in. The very smell of it made Alfie wake up and we all ate our fill.

It was strange, knowing for certain that Lady Margaret was our grandma. It turned out that Sir Samuel had died sudden three weeks before.

'I'm sorry that Sir Samuel died,' I said not sure if I was saying the right thing.

She looked sad for a minute but then a smile crossed her face. 'I am sorry too, Sam. I'm sorry he is not here to see you fine children. But I shall do my best for you and I'm sure it's what your grandfather would want.'

I don't have to tell you how glad we were that things turned out so jammy. We were as happy as a dog with two tails. We could hardly believe we'd found Pa and Grandma all in the same day. Even Patch was running round in circles, woofing at chair legs and diving under the sideboard.

When we had finished our breakfast, Grandma called for Bridget. 'You were quite right to bring me that letter,' she said. 'I've been a foolish old woman and I'm asking you to forgive my rudeness. Will you stay and look after the children?'

'Oh, I will, madam. I will gladly,' she said giving a kind of a curtsey and smiling from ear to ear.

'Then please prepare the bath for them,' she said. 'Wetherby will help you.'

For the next half an hour the two of them ran up and down the stairs carrying pails of hot water. It must have been hard work. Then, when Bridget said the bath was ready, she lifted Alfie just in case he wasn't up to climbing stairs.

We were surprised that toffs had baths upstairs. It seemed silly to us. At home with Ma and Pa, our tin bath hung outside on the wall, see. Every Saturday we'd carry it indoors, fill it with hot water from the kettle and then wash in front of the fire. That was cosy, that was.

This was different. For a start, the bath was huge! It wasn't made of tin, like ours – it was made of copper and set in a fine wooden cabinet in a room as big as a house. I didn't seem right to me. And when Bridget said we had to take our clothes off and rub ourselves all over with soap that smelled of lavender or something, I said, 'Do we have to?' But Bridget said, yes, we did.

The bath was so big we all climbed in together. At least that was a laugh. We were soaking in hot water for ages and it wasn't as bad as I thought. We stayed till our skin turned pink and wrinkly and our hair changed to coppery red while the water turned grey with the dirt. I don't think I'd realised how dirty we were.

'You can get out now,' said Bridget, lifting Alfie first and wrapping him in a white towel and rubbing him dry.

Our muddy clothes had been taken away and we were all given a blanket to wrap round us and we stood by the bath looking like right goosecaps, laughing and giggling.

'Lady Margaret will buy you new clothes, I'm sure,' said Bridget. 'And what about Patch? Shall we dip him in the water, do you think?'

We thought it was a good idea and she lifted him in the bath. He didn't seem to mind at all – except when he got out and shook himself dry, he showered the whole room and everybody in it.

Forty-One

Explanations

That evening, Pa came downstairs looking much better. Not quite as pale. A little bit steadier on his feet.

Grandma was pleased. 'The sight of your children was the best medicine in the world, my dear,' she said. 'Come. Let us all sit in the parlour by the fire so we can talk.'

We went into another big room with high ceilings and oil lamps everywhere and a fire roaring in the grate. Patch flopped down on the rug by the hearth and fell asleep straight away while the four of us sat on a huge velvet settee. Pa had Alfie on his lap, Eliza sat on one side and I sat on the other. Cosy, it was.

'Well,' said Grandma, settled in a small armchair, 'I can see that things are going to change around Blythfield Hall. And I'm looking forward to it, I must say. I've been without my family for far too long.' She leaned forward. 'I've been a wicked woman.'

'You don't look wicked,' said Alfie.

Grandma smiled. 'Maybe not. But your grandpa and I did a wicked thing when we disowned your father.'

'What's disowned?'

'We sent him away, Alfie. We said we would never speak to him again.'

'Why did you do that?' asked Alfie, which is what we all wanted to know but didn't like to ask.

Grandma sighed. 'We wanted your father to marry a rich girl, you see. Someone from a good family. We didn't think your mother was suitable. She was poor and we didn't like that.'

It was hard to believe Pa grew up in a rich family and in a house like this.

'Ma couldn't help being poor,' said Alfie.

'I know that now, Alfie, but I was foolish then. I sent your father away and didn't see him again until two weeks ago, the week after my husband died. I couldn't believe that, after such sadness, there would come such joy. Your father came to my door asking for help.'

Eliza grinned. 'You didn't send him away that time, did you, Grandma?'

She laughed. 'How good it is to hear you call me Grandma. I regret not knowing you for all those years. Can you forgive me?'

Alfie slipped off the settee and climbed up onto Grandma's lap. 'Do you like having us here then?' he asked. 'Can we stay if we're good?'

Grandma tweaked Alfie's nose and smiled. 'You can only stay if Patch stays too,' she said. 'There are lots of rats that need catching.' Which pleased Alfie no end.

Just then, Bridget came and set up a little table by the fire.

'Missus O'Leary's made some cakes special,' she said. 'She's put strawberry jam and cream in 'em.' She bustled out and returned a few minutes later with a tray piled with cups and saucers and plates of scones and a large sponge cake. 'Missus O'Leary says she hopes there won't be a crumb left by the time you've had your tea or she'll want to know the reason why,' and she winked before walking out of the room.

We didn't want to disappoint Missus O'Leary and so we did our best and ate all the scones and two slices of cake each. When we'd finished we sank back feeling very full and happy to be with our family.

'Tell us what happened in America, Pa,' I said. 'Did you make lots of money?'

He shook his head. 'I worked hard in the sweltering heat but then I grew sick with the fever. I was ill for a long time and what I'd earned was almost spent on doctors. I was desperate to get back to you and with the last of my money, I got on a boat to Liverpool. Then I had to walk the rest of the way home.'

'But we weren't there, were we, Pa?' said Alfie.

Pa looked sad. 'No, you were gone.'

'Did you see our letter pinned to the door?' Eliza asked.

But Pa shook his head. 'It must have blown away, Eliza,' he said. 'I found out Ma had died from some neighbours. They told me you were living with Aunt Maud and Uncle Bert in Camden.'

The three of us sat and nodded, remembering how we'd left our home in the cart.

'When I got there, Uncle Bert's shop was closed and nobody knew where you were. By then, I was so ill that I came back to Blythfield Hall to ask my parents for help.'

'Aunt Maud was nice,' said Alfie. 'But we didn't like Uncle Bert. He was mean.'

Pa put his arm round Alfie. 'Well, it's all over now, son,' he said, squeezing him tight. 'Grandma will look after us all now.'

Alfie clapped his hands. 'Three cheers for Grandma,' he called and we set about cheering loud enough to be heard in the kitchen.

But I could tell Eliza wasn't happy. She went and stood with her back to the fire, facing us. 'It's all very well,' she said. 'We're ever so lucky, full of cake and sitting by a nice warm fire. But only last night we were locked in that room at Blythwell Hall.'

Eliza was right and she made me think of all the boys still starving and cold.

'Grandma,' I said. 'Can we do something to help Dembow? He was one of the boys at Blythwell Hall. He helped us escape.'

'And what about the others?' said Eliza. 'They're kept like prisoners by them Mogwurts.'

Grandma frowned. 'Blythwell Hall? Why that's just a few miles from here. What are you talking about? Tell me. And who are these Mogwurts?'

So we told her how we came to be at that terrible school.

'Good heavens!' said Grandma, banging her hand on the arm of the chair. 'That is quite disgraceful.'

'Indeed it is,' said Pa who was just as angry. 'The Mogwurts are making money out of children's misery.'

Grandma stood up. 'I shall get this dreadful place closed down,' she said. 'I shall see to it that the Mogwurts are brought before the magistrate as soon as possible.'

Forty-Two

The answer to a problem

Grandma was true to her word. She got busy writing letters and a magistrate, who was a friend of hers, came up to the house and talked about what should be done. We were asked to speak to him as we were the experts, as you might say. So we told him what Blythwell Hall was like and he sat and listened and nodded.

'Well,' he said. 'That's a very sad tale. But I think there will be no problem in shutting down Blythwell Hall.'

'Wonderful!' said Grandma. 'I'm sure you're all pleased about that, aren't you?'

Of course we were. 'But what happens to Dembow and the other kids?' I asked her. 'Where they going to go? You won't send 'em to the workhouse, will yer?'

'No indeed,' she replied. 'You said there were fourteen children?'

'About that.'

Grandma smiled. 'This is a big house. There are bedrooms on the top floor that only need a fresh coat of paint and some beds – but there will be enough room for fourteen children.' And of course we cheered and bounced up and hugged Grandma.

The magistrate was not so sure. 'Margaret,' he said. 'You are not a young woman and this is a great deal of responsibility. You can't have them in your house. What will they do all day?'

Pa, who was looking so much better, said, 'I have an idea, Mother. There are barns on the estate. We could turn them into classrooms and I would be very happy to teach the children.'

'Pa can read,' said Eliza. 'He taught us to write, he did. He would be a brilliant teacher.'

Grandma seemed pleased with the idea. She looked at the magistrate and shook her head. 'I'm not too old to have a dream,' she said. 'I have a good deal of money and I shall make this my life's work to make up for the wrong I've done.'

It happened very quickly. We all got very busy and had a grand time painting the walls of the bedrooms. In less than a week, fourteen new beds arrived and we were real excited.

By the next week, the school at Blythwell Hall was shut down and the Mogwurts were put in prison waiting to be sent to trial.

That was when the fun started. All the kids were brought up to Grandma's house on a cart and we went running out to meet them. There was Dembow waving and grinning. It was so good to see him again.

'Well, you took yer time,' he said, cheeky as ever. 'Thought you'd forgotten us.'

He jumped down off the cart and looked at the house. 'Still, you did us proud. I never thought I'd stay in a place like this. Thanks, matey.'

'Why have we come here?' asked little Jimmie, shaking with fright. 'Will I have to clean them chimneys?'

'No,' said Alfie. 'You can live with us and I'll be your friend.' And from then on he looked after the poor mite.

Everything worked out well. Grandma put an extra table in the dining room. Missus O'Leary did lots of cooking so all of us kids were soon as plump as a Christmas goose. Pa got well and strong and started teaching us in the barns though there were times when he was sad and he talked of Ma.

'I'm sad she got sick,' he'd say. 'And I wish she could see you now. She'd be so proud of you. Three brave, clever children.'

But Alfie insisted Ma could see us. 'Don't you know, Pa? She's looking down and watching us all the time to make sure we're being good.'

And that made Pa feel better.

Grandma taught some of us to play the piano and we all learned songs, though Eliza had the sweetest voice of any of us.

Alfie and Jimmie got friendly with the gamekeeper and walked round the woods with him and his dog, Bonny. Patch and Bonny were good friends, too, but it was quite a surprise when Bonny had four bootiful pups.

'I'll look after 'em,' Alfie said to Grandma. 'They're Patch's babies, aren't they? They're family – just like you and me.'

Grandma could never say no to any of us. 'If you promise to take care of them, Alfie, you can keep them,' she said and she smiled her lovely smile which grew better every day. 'I know now. There's nothing so important as family.'

And we had to agree.